About the author

David Fuller is an FA
currently coaches a y
He has worked as a j
during which time he
publications on a vai
lives in Newhaven, East
sons and cat Merry.

CW00867703

Other books by David Fuller

Alfie Jones and a change of fortune
Alfie Jones and a test of character

To Ben and Lucy

RDF Publishing
3 Courtlands Mews, Church Hill, Newhaven,
East Sussex,
BN9 9LU

Alfie Jones and the missing link
A RDF Publishing book

First published in Great Britain by RDF Publishing in 2013
Printed and bound in the UK by Berforts Information Press,
King's Lynn.

1
Text copyright © David Fuller
Images courtesy of Rob Smyth
(http://reactors-on.blogspot.com)

ISBN 978-0-9570339-2-4

For more exclusive Alfie Jones content, visit:
www.alfie-jones.co.uk

ALFIE JONES AND THE MISSING LINK

DAVID FULLER

Illustrated by
Rob Smyth

www.alfie-jones.co.uk

Chapter one

The excitement had been building from the moment they stepped off the train. Now, as Alfie Jones and his four friends caught their first glimpse of the Stanton Road stadium, their spirits soared to a new level of exuberance.

Stanton Road was the home of Kingsway United – Alfie's favourite professional football team, who played in League One. Although Alfie had seen the stadium many, many times before – his parents drove past it whenever they went to his Nan's house – today was different. Today Alfie was actually going to be watching a real game there. Live.

"Excited, Alf?" asked Alfie's best friend Billy Morris, as the group quickly made their way past the vast assortment of burger vans and stalls selling Kingsway United-related merchandise that always lined the streets surrounding the stadium on match days.

Alfie nodded enthusiastically, but couldn't stop himself from looking at his best buddy like he was a little mad. What kind of a stupid question was that to ask? Of course he was excited. In fact, he doubted he'd ever felt so excited in his entire life.

He was finally going to get to see his heroes play football up close!

The trip to Stanton Road for the match between Kingsway United and Portland City had been organised by Liam Walker's parents as part of Liam's tenth birthday celebrations. Alfie, Billy and Liam all played for the Kingsway Colts under 10s and they, along with fellow Colts' teammates Hayden Whitlock and Chloe Reed, had been looking forward to the match for weeks.

Liam had seen United play at Stanton Road on a number of occasions before, but for the other four this would be their first live Kingsway United match – although Hayden had previously held a season ticket for League Two side Norton Town,

until he'd moved to Kingsway prior to the start of the current season.

There was still well over an hour until the match was due to kick off, but all five children had wanted to get to the ground early so that they would have plenty of time to look around the club shop. Liam had his Birthday money to spend, while the others had been saving their pocket money from the moment they had been told they would be going to the match. Luckily, Mr Walker, who was taking the children, had happily agreed to the children's demands to arrive early.

As the five friends and teammates approached the large blue and white-painted portable building which served as United's club shop, Alfie was still trying to decide how he was going to spend the £20 he'd managed to save. Although he had never been inside the club shop before, he had spent hours on Kingsway United's official website, pouring over all the various goods you could buy.

What he really wanted was a new replica shirt, but he knew that he didn't have enough money for one. For now he'd have to make do with having last season's shirt, which he was at that very moment proudly wearing over a blue sweater so that everyone could see he was decked out in Kingsway United's famous blue and white stripes.

The inside of the club shop was better than anything Alfie could ever have hoped for. Every bit of available space in the portable building had been crammed with various Kingsway United goods. There were blue and white scarves and bobble hats proudly sporting Kingsway United's badge – a king's crown sitting atop a castle's turret. There were replica shirts and training tops. There were Kingsway United pin badges, car stickers, air fresheners, team posters, alarm clocks, coffee mugs, baby bottles...

4

There were even soft toy versions of United's mascot, Royal Joe – a crown-wearing lion, dressed in a Kingsway United kit. Alfie knew he wouldn't be buying one of those, though. He already had his own lucky mascot – a football kit wearing-teddy bear which had been given to him by a mysterious fortune teller over a year ago.

After spending around ten minutes agonising over what to spend his money on, Alfie finally decided to buy a scarf, some pin badges and an alarm clock. Having chosen exactly which badges and alarm clock he wanted, Alfie was in the middle of discussing with Billy and Hayden – both of whom had already brought their treats – just what scarf he should buy, when the three friends heard a familiar, sneering voice.

"Well, well, well, if it isn't the three loser-teers."

They didn't need to turn round to see who was speaking to them.

It was Jasper Johnson. They'd recognise his mocking voice anywhere.

Jasper went to the same junior school as the three boys and had, for a short time, once been a Kingsway Colts player. Although this was before Hayden had joined the team, the newest addition to the Colts had himself played alongside Jasper in a six-a-side tournament before the start of the season. It hadn't been a particularly pleasant experience.

"What do you want Jasper?" Alfie asked angrily, without taking his eyes away from the scarf rail.

"What do I want from you, muppet? Absolutely nothing – what could you possibly give me? I just thought it would be nice for the three of you to be seen talking to a real-life superstar!"

The three boys turned to face their former teammate. Jasper was wearing a full Kingsway United training kit. However, Alfie, Billy and Hayden knew only too well that this particular tracksuit could not be purchased in the club shop.

This was special training gear that was only given to players lucky enough to be selected for the Kingsway United Academy.

Before the start of the season, to almost everyone's shock, Jasper had been invited for trials at United's Elite Centre – which he had passed. If this wasn't surprising enough, Jasper was then selected to join the club's academy, which was attended by only the most talented players in the entire Kingsway area.

If there was one thing Jasper most certainly wasn't, it was a talented football player. His main asset, his only asset in fact, was his power – Jasper was far bigger and a lot stronger than most boys his own age – but in terms of football ability he was nothing special. Billy and, especially, Hayden were far better players, while Alfie himself was a lot more skilful. Yet none of them had ever been invited to try out for the Elite Centre, let alone the Academy.

In recent months, Jasper had become cockier than ever. He had stopped playing football at school break times as he refused "to play with muppets who are nowhere near as talented as me," while he was no longer allowed to play for North Malling Town – the team his dad, Keith, coached – due to his Academy commitments. Put simply, Jasper had become completely unbearable.

"So, which one of you wants my autograph first?" Jasper continued, clearly believing that he was already a professional footballer.

"Go away, Jasper," said Billy. "You're not as great as you think you are."

Jasper laughed. "You're just jealous," he said turning away from the three friends. "You'd do anything to be in the Academy like I am. See you later, losers."

These words stung Alfie, Billy and Hayden more than Jasper could ever have hoped. As, for possibly the first time in his entire life, the larger boy was 100 per cent correct. All three boys would do almost anything to be in the Kingsway United Academy and they were all jealous of him.

"I really don't understand it," said Alfie, after Jasper had finally sauntered off out of view. "You two are both far better than he is. What do the Academy coaches see in him?"

"My Dad reckons Keith must be involved somehow," remarked Billy.

"He must be," agreed Hayden. "He was going to get me a trial, remember... until I decided that I didn't want to join his team."

"But how can Keith have anything to do with Kingsway United? He's still coaching North Malling."

Hayden and Billy shrugged their shoulders. Neither boy could think of an answer that would make any sense.

Suddenly Chloe and Liam came running

over to join their friends. "Hurry-up you three," exclaimed Liam. "The match starts in 20 minutes and you still haven't joined the queue yet, Alfie. It's quite long and we don't want to miss the kick off."

Without saying another word, Alfie yanked the closest scarf from the rail and rushed over to join the queue.

While he was standing in the line waiting to be served, Alfie saw Jasper walking past the door of the club shop. He was laughing and joking with some of the other Academy players. There was something not quite right about Jasper's involvement with the Kingsway United Academy, yet Alfie didn't have the slightest idea what his former teammate could be doing to influence his selection.

But if there was one thing Alfie did know, it was that he was going to do all he could to find out just what was going on.

Chapter two

Although the ground was far from full,
Alfie was amazed by just how much noise
roughly 6,000 football fans could make.
He'd watched hundreds of matches on
the television but nothing could have
prepared him for the electrifying sound
produced by the roar of a real-life football
crowd.

He and his friends had contributed
with much enthusiasm towards that
noise. They had started singing from the
moment they had found their seats and
as the referee blew his whistle for half-
time they'd hardly so much as paused for
breath.

And there was plenty for them to sing
about. United had stormed into a 3-0 first

half lead, with Hugo Becker – Alfie's hero – in particularly fine form, having scored the team's first two goals and then set up the third.

"Wow. This is so amazing!" proclaimed Alfie excitedly, as the group of friends waited for the second half to begin. "How good is Becker!"

"I've never seen him play this well before," admitted Liam, whose own favourite player, Harry Simpson, had scored United's other goal. "You must be Becker's lucky mascot, Alfie. You should come more often."

"I wish I could. I'd love to come and watch every week. That'd be so cool!"

"Yeah, I know," agreed Liam. "Dad said he might try and get me a season ticket next year. You should see if your Mum and Dad will get you one."

"Yeah. Maybe," Alfie replied, without much enthusiasm.

Although he couldn't imagine anything better than owning a Kingsway United season ticket, Alfie didn't think that there was any chance he'd be allowed to get one. For a start he wouldn't have anyone to take him to the games. His parents didn't have any interest in football whatsoever, and instead tended to spend their weekends taking his younger sister, Megan, to her latest fad; street dance.

He already relied on Billy's dad to get him to and from Colts' training and matches every Saturday and Sunday, and so until he was old enough to get the train by himself he figured owning a season ticket would remain little more than a dream.

The five friends continued to talk amongst themselves for a while, chatting about what they thought would happen in the second half and about the Colts' own game against Danehill United the following day, when their conversation was interrupted by a voice coming from a speaker located directly above their heads.

"We've got some very special Birthday messages to read out," declared the match day announcer. "First off, it's a very happy 10th Birthday to Liam Walker who is sitting in the Kingsway Road stand today with his Dad and four of his Kingsway Colts under 10s teammates. Liam's favourite player is Harry Simpson and this is his ninth visit to Stanton Road. I'm sure Liam and his friends have thoroughly enjoyed that first half performance from the lads."

Alfie, Hayden, Billy and Chloe cheered
and whooped as loudly as they possibly
could, while Liam blushed and tried to
hide his embarrassment (and also his
secret pleasure) at hearing his name read
out.

After reading out another three
Birthday messages, the announcer then
ran through some of the half-time scores
from other games taking place that
afternoon. The news that league leaders
Merseywood Town were losing 2-1 away
to Leston Athletic was also met with
much glee by Alfie and his buddies.

"And before the players come out for the
second half," continued the announcer,
"please put your hands together for the
boys from the Kingsway United under
10s Academy who are going to give you a
sneak preview of some of the silky skills
you may be witnessing here at Stanton
Road in a few year's time."

The Colts' teammates all exchanged
uneasy glances. Seconds later their worst
fears were realised. There, emerging
out of the players' tunnel, dressed in full
Kingsway United kit, was Jasper.

Their former teammate skipped out
onto the Stanton Road pitch, bending
down to pick up some grass as he went.

He greeted the warm applause he and his fellow Academy players were receiving from the United fans by waving vigorously back at them before placing his hands over his head to clap the crowd back. Most of the crowd loved the antics of the large boy, who looked more like an under 13 than an under 10, and began to clap even louder, prompting Jasper to give them a double thumbs up.

Not all the crowd were so amused, though. "Anyone would think he's already a superstar the way he's carrying on," moaned Billy, unable to keep the jealousy from his voice.

"I can't believe what I'm seeing," responded Liam. "This has to be a nightmare... either that or a really bad joke!"

It was no joke, though. Jasper really was just about to get to play football in front of a crowd at Stanton Road.

The exercise the Academy players were going to be performing was a straightforward shooting drill. They were to line up just outside the penalty area and pass a ball into the coach's feet who would then lay it back to the player to shoot first time.

The first player to shoot wowed the

crowd by bending the ball with his right foot into the top left-hand corner of the goal. He received a standing ovation and even Billy had to admit that it was a great shot.

The next four boys to try their luck were not so impressive. Although two of them scored, that owed more to poor goalkeeping than it did to good shooting, while the other two players skewed their efforts horribly wide.

Then it was Jasper's turn to shoot. All five Colts' players had their fingers crossed, hoping that Jasper would mess up.

They weren't to be disappointed.

Jasper's pass to the coach was simply dreadful, landing closer to the corner flag than to the intended recipient's feet. Alfie and his friends burst out laughing, only to be moaned at by a group of men sitting behind them, who told the Colts' players to "leave the big guy alone. He's probably just a bit nervous."

The friends stifled their giggles and then watched eagerly as Jasper began a second attempt to make a simple ten yard pass. This time the pass was fine, but when the ball was then rolled back towards him, he completely failed to connect with it, kicking at air rather than the ball.

A gentle ripple of laughter, mixed with some sympathetic murmurings, started to echo around the stadium, and even the group of men sitting behind Alfie and his friends couldn't help but chuckle.

Even from where he was sitting, Alfie could see that Jasper's face was starting to go beetroot red – something which always happened when he got angry; which was fairly regularly. The coach signalled to Jasper that he would have one more chance. Jasper took a deep breath and played another decent pass into the coach's feet. The ball came back to him and, finally, Jasper managed to get a shot away. However, while there could be no doubting the shot's power, which was simply frightening for a ten year old, the accuracy left a lot to be desired and the ball not only cleared the crossbar, but flew high up into the stand behind the goal, narrowly missing the face of an unsuspecting supporter.

Jasper stared hard at the coach, suggesting the miss-hit shot was somehow his fault, and then stormed off to the back of the line – his big moment ruined.

"Same old Jasper," said Chloe, desperately trying not to laugh.

"I still don't get how he's in the Academy," Billy wondered aloud. "Still, that was funny wasn't it, Alf."

But Alfie wasn't listening to his friends. His attention had been caught by two men who were standing on the side of the pitch by the player's tunnel.

Although he didn't recognise one of the men, dressed in the same Kingsway United training kit that Jasper had been wearing in the club shop, the second man he knew only too well. It was Jasper's Dad, Keith, who for a short time had been the Colts' coach and had made Alfie's life a misery.

The two men were engaged in what appeared to Alfie to be a serious conversation. At first Keith had looked angry, but by the time the two men had finished talking he was smiling from ear to ear. He patted the mystery man on the back and then climbed over an advertising board before sitting down in a seat located in the main stand just behind the manager's dug-outs. The man in the training kit, meanwhile, headed back down the tunnel and was soon out of Alfie's sight.

Alfie couldn't help but feel that what Billy had said in the club shop a little earlier must somehow be right. Keith really must have had something to do with Jasper being selected for the Academy.

But what?

Chapter three

It seemed to Alfie like he and his friends had been queuing for ages to get onto the train.

The Stanton Road stadium was located just a ten-minute walk from the train station, and as there were not many free car parking spaces available on the roads that surrounded the ground, the majority of supporters who attended Kingsway United matches tended to travel by train.

Liam's Dad had tentatively suggested leaving the game a few minutes early in an attempt to beat the queues which always built up on the approach to the train station on match days. But all five of the Colts' players had refused to budge from their seats until the referee had blown the final whistle and they'd been able to clap their heroes off the pitch.

There was then a further delay as, halfway to the station, Liam decided that he did need to go to the toilet after all, and the group had to troop all the way back to the stadium so that the birthday boy could ensure there would not be any unwanted accidents on the journey home.

Therefore, by the time the friends approached the station on that cold early February evening, a considerable queue had already formed and they had to wait a good half-hour before they were even allowed onto the platform, as numerous trains came and went taking other United supporters on their way home.

However, in spite of the wintry chill in the air, none of the children were complaining about the lengthy wait. Kingsway United had ended up running out comfortable 5-0 winners – their biggest win of the season. Harry Simpson had wrapped up the scoring in the final minute of injury time, completing his hat-trick in the process. The five children took great delight in constantly reminding Mr Walker that they would have missed the last goal if they'd followed his advice and left early.

Finally, almost 50 minutes after they had originally joined the queue outside the station, their train arrived. Thankfully, as they were among the last supporters left waiting on the platform, there were plenty of available seats on the train and Alfie and his friends, along with Liam's Dad, settled down for the short journey to Kingsway train station.

All five Colts' players had thoroughly enjoyed the match and were all suffering with slightly sore throats from cheering and singing so much. But there was little doubt about what the highlight of the day had been for all of them – Jasper making a complete fool of himself.

The children couldn't stop themselves from laughing as Liam recreated Jasper's air-kick in the aisle of the near-empty train. Even his Dad joined in with the fun, pretending to be the person in the crowd who the ball had so very nearly hit in the face once Jasper had finally managed to kick it.

All the talk of Jasper had reminded Alfie of a question he'd been wanting to ask his friends, and once the giggling and general hilarity had subsided, he inquired as to whether anyone else had seen Keith speaking to the man by the player's tunnel during the half-time interval.

None of them had.

Alfie outlined exactly what he had witnessed.

"I knew it," exclaimed Billy the moment Alfie had finished telling his story. "Keith's definitely got something to do with Jasper being picked for the Academy. Why else would he have been speaking to that man? I mean, the other man must be something to do with Kingsway United if he was wearing the training kit and was allowed to walk back down the tunnel."

Alfie, Hayden and Liam all nodded their agreement. Then, the four boys all looked at Chloe, who was looking a little puzzled.

"What's up, Chloe?" asked Alfie. "Do you not think Keith must be behind Jasper being picked for the Academy?"

"It's not that. He probably is," Chloe answered. "But... well... thinking about it, there's something else that's a bit weird about this whole Academy thingy."

The four boys all leaned forward, interested to hear what their only female teammate had to say. Even Liam's Dad lowered the newspaper he was reading as a signal that he too was listening to her.

"It's just that," Chloe continued, "Well... none of the other Academy players seemed that good either. Well, aside from that first boy who curled his shot into the top corner, and maybe a couple of others who had quite good shots. Everyone else, though, was... well... a little bit rubbish. Don't you think? Even the goalkeeper."

There was a short period of silence as the four boys thought about what Chloe had said. It was Liam's Dad who was the first to speak.

"They could have just been nervous," he suggested. "Imagine how you lot would feel if you suddenly had to shoot at goal in front of thousands of people. It can't be easy. I'd certainly be nervous."

"Maybe. Yeah, you're probably right," conceded Chloe. "I just thought it was a bit, well... odd."

"I don't think I'd be nervous," said Liam, confidently. "I would have stuck it in the top corner with my eyes closed and using my left foot!"

"You can't even do that in the back garden, son, let alone in front of a big crowd," said Mr Walker, punching Liam affectionately on the arm.

Everyone laughed. Even Liam, although

perhaps not quite as loudly as the others. However, all four boys still couldn't stop themselves from thinking about what Chloe had said. Nervous or not, all the Colts' players thought they could have produced far better shots than most of the Academy players had been able to muster.

"So how do we find out who that man who was talking to Keith is?" asked Alfie, after a while.

"Why?" Hayden and Liam responded together.

"I don't really know," admitted Alfie. "I just think that if we find out who he is, then we might find out more about why Jasper is in the Academy and you aren't." Although Alfie gestured at all three boys when he said this, he was only really talking about Billy and Hayden. Liam scored loads of goals, but Alfie didn't really think his friend was any better than he was in terms of football ability, whereas the other two were both on a different level. He didn't want to upset Liam by leaving him out, though.

However, before anyone had the chance to make any suggestions regarding how they could go about discovering the identity of the mystery man, the train pulled into Kingsway Station.

"Up you get then boys and girl," said Mr Walker, ushering the children off their seats. "Make sure you've got everything with you. It would be a shame to leave any of your new things on the train."

Billy, Chloe and Hayden were all being picked up at the station, and due to the longer than expected wait for a train, their parents had already been waiting for them for quite a while by the time they stepped onto the platform.

The three friends thanked Liam and his Dad for a great day, and then went their separate ways home. Alfie, however, would be walking home with Liam and Mr Walker.

As his parents had been at a street dance rehearsal with Megan all day, they'd said that getting to the station in time to pick him up could prove to be a problem. As it turned out, they would have had plenty of time to get there, but they weren't to know that when they had originally made plans with Liam's Dad.

The two boys spent most of the walk to Alfie's house talking about the Colts' following day's game against Danehill United. Not once did they mention Jasper or the Kingsway United Academy.

They had just turned the corner into the road in which Alfie lived, when he suddenly stopped walking and stood rooted to the spot, as still as a statue.

"Are you alright?" asked Liam, wondering why, out of the blue, his friend had just decided to stop moving. "What's the matter?"

"Shhh," said Alfie, trying desperately to hush his friend. "Did you hear someone call my name?" he whispered after a short period of silence.

"No, I didn't hear anything. Did you Dad?"

Mr Walker shook his head. "Nope. Sorry Alfie. I didn't hear anything, either."

Alfie stood motionless for a moment longer, hoping that the faint voice that he was certain he'd just heard say his name would call out again. It didn't.

"I must be hearing things," he said aloud, convinced that he must indeed have been mistaken.

He ran to catch up with Liam again when a sudden sound made him jump.

"What's that!" Alfie exclaimed excitedly, a look of, firstly, shock and then pure elation spreading across his face.

"Calm down, Alfie," said Liam, laughing. "It's just a wind chime. I'm sure you must have heard a wind chime before. It's nothing to get excited about."

Liam was both right and wrong.

He was right in that Alfie had indeed heard the gentle jingle jangle of a wind chime before – and, more often than not, the deafening din made by lots of wind chimes clanging at the same time. On many occasions, in fact.

Where Liam was wrong, though, was that in Alfie's experience, the sound of a wind chime was usually something to get very excited about!

Chapter four

It had all started at a pre-Christmas fun-fair some 14 months earlier. Alfie had been waiting for Megan to finish her fourth ride on a merry-go-round when he had suddenly heard a voice saying his name. A quick search of the surrounding area had not revealed the identity of the person that had been calling him, but Alfie's attention was captured by the sight of a fortune teller's tent – or, to be more specific, by the fact his name was written on a blackboard located directly outside the tent.

Upon entering the tent, Alfie had been disappointed to find it empty and had been just about to leave when a bunch of wind chimes, which had been hanging from the ceiling, started chiming. Before Alfie even had time to think about what was happening the tent had filled with smoke and when it cleared just moments later, a fortune teller called Madam Zola was standing in front of him.

It quickly became apparent to Alfie that Madam Zola was no ordinary fortune teller as she knew simply everything there was to know about him. More excitingly, though, she told the young boy that he would one day become a professional football player – providing he listened to her advice and kept their meetings a secret.

Since then, he had met the fortune teller on a handful of occasions. Indeed, it was largely thanks to Madam Zola that he had become friends with Hayden.

All of these encounters, except for one, had been preceded by the sound of wind chimes. Therefore, on this particular evening, when Alfie heard wind chimes so soon after believing someone had been calling his name, he was positive that Madam Zola must be close by.

However, it was now almost his bed-time, and much to his annoyance no further strange incidents had occurred.

"I thought you'd be in a better mood this

evening after the Kingsway United game today," noted Mr Jones, as Alfie mooched up the stairs to clean his teeth. "Me and your Mum have never seen you as excited as you were when you got home from the game."

Alfie just shrugged his shoulders and grunted something about being tired. He couldn't tell his Dad the real reason that he was so irritated was due to the fact Madam Zola hadn't shown up yet. He knew that he shouldn't to talk to anyone about her, and was also aware that even if he did he risked whoever he decided to tell thinking him to be completely crazy.

Unsurprisingly, with the buzz of that day's Kingsway United game, the excitement of the Colts' match the following morning and thoughts of perhaps seeing Madam Zola all filling his head, Alfie struggled to get to sleep that night.

After about an hour of constant tossing and turning, Alfie had finally begun to drift off when there was a sudden loud knock on his bedroom door.

"Hello," said Alfie, uncertainly, while slowly propping himself up on his elbows. There was no answer.

"Hello," he called out again, a little

louder this time. Once more, though, no answer was forthcoming.

Convinced he must either have been mistaken or that Megan was playing silly games, Alfie settled back down in his bed to try and get to sleep. However, as soon as his head hit the pillow, there came yet another knock at the door.

'Right, that's it,' Alfie said silently to himself, fairly certain it was his little sister playing silly tricks. 'I'll show her.'

Alfie rolled out of his bed as quietly as he could and crept slowly towards the door, taking extra care not to trip over one of the many piles of football magazines, cards or lego bricks which littered his bedroom floor.

His plan was to fling the door open and then roar at his sibling using his best monster voice. He knew that Megan still occasionally had night terrors regarding monsters hiding in the wardrobe and was relishing the look of utter horror on her face when he roared at her. He knew it was a cruel trick but figured that, as she'd started it by knocking on his door while he was trying to sleep, it would be her own fault when she screamed.

He stifled a giggle as he placed his left hand on the door handle and started to slowly apply some downward pressure. Then, quick as a flash, he flung the door wide open and was just about to roar when, for the second time in the space of only a few hours, something made him freeze.

Megan wasn't standing in front of him. In fact, no one was.

However, when Alfie had gone to bed earlier that evening he'd been pretty sure that there hadn't been a tree situated on either side of his bedroom door. He was also pretty sure that the upstairs hallway had had a ceiling and walls.

Well it didn't anymore.

Alfie looked behind him and could see that everything in his bedroom was just as it should be. Football posters still adorned the walls, magazines were still scattered in hastily made piles across the floor, lego bricks were still strewn everywhere, and there were most certainly four walls and a ceiling.

He looked out of the door again. All he could see were trees.

He was tempted to run back into his room, shut the door and hide under the covers, but instead he stepped out of his bedroom door into what should have been the upstairs hallway.

"Ouch," shouted Alfie at the top of his voice as he stood on what he thought must be a toy. However, upon looking at the ground he realised there were no toys lying around. There were, though, plenty of twigs, leaves and branches.

Alfie rubbed his eyes and reached for where he knew the hallway light switch to be. Instead of turning on a light, however, Alfie merely found himself pressing his fingers up against the wet bark of a tree.

He knew that he should have been terrified. He knew that he should scream for his parents... or even Megan. But something inside Alfie prevented him from doing this. Instead, he began to slowly start walking along the cool, moist, twig- and leaf-strewn path where the landing should have been.

In the dim light the young boy couldn't believe what he was seeing, but there could be no doubt about it. He was walking in some kind of wood. He could hear the bubbling of a nearby stream, the sound of birds chirping, while all around him all he could see were trees and bushes of all different shapes and sizes.

Suddenly Alfie heard something rustling in some nearby shrubbery.

He walked cautiously over to where the noise was coming from and carefully parted some leaves. Quick as a flash something jumped out at Alfie, causing his heart to race so fast that it felt as though it might explode. It was like bullets were repeatedly firing against his chest from the inside. He was just about to let out an almighty scream when, through the corner of one of his eyes, he glimpsed what it was that had leapt out at him from the bush.

"It's only a squirrel. There's nothing to be scared of," Alfie whispered loudly, trying to convince himself that he needn't be afraid. He took three deep breaths to try and settle himself, when he suddenly heard the same knocking noise that he'd heard back in his bedroom.

The sound of the knocking was coming from back in the direction he had just walked from. This time, though, it wasn't just one single knock, it was repeating, urgent-sounding, banging.

He turned to follow the sound and moments later found himself back at his bedroom door. The knocking, by now, was extremely loud and he could also clearly hear voices calling his name.

Alfie ran back into his bedroom and

did what he figured he should have done some minutes earlier. He slammed the door shut and turned on the light.

However, the knocking did not stop and the voices calling his name only grew louder and louder. Alfie flung the door open again and readied himself to scream at the top of his voice for his parents.

But he didn't have to bother.

Because when the door was open, standing in front of him were his Mum and Dad.

"Morning sleepy head," said Mrs Jones, affectionately. "I didn't think you were ever going to wake up this morning."

Alfie rubbed at his eyes again before peering past his parents, expecting to see trees. However, he could immediately see that everything was back to normal. 'It was just a dream,' he thought to himself, letting out a huge sigh of relief.

"Are you okay, Alf?" asked Mr Jones. "You're acting very strangely."

"Yep, I'm fine," said Alfie, whilst shaking his head frantically from side-to-side, as if by doing so he could shake the weird dream from his memory.

"Well get a move on, sweetie," continued Mrs Jones. "Billy and his Dad will be here in a little while to take you to football.

I've never known you sleep in so late on a Sunday when you've got a football match. You're normally up hours before, bouncing off the walls with excitement. I even had to double check the calendar to make sure you had a game."

"Just give me a minute to find my kit," replied a still very dazed and confused Alfie, before turning to go off in search of his football stuff.

"Is your foot okay, Alf?" Mr Jones asked, noticing that his son was limping slightly.

"Yeah it feels fine. Why?"

"It's just that you're limping slightly. And... yes... it looks like the bottom of your right foot is bleeding a little."

Baffled, Alfie sat down on the floor so that he could easier examine the bottom of his foot to see what his Dad was talking about.

Sure enough, there was a tiny spot of blood in the centre of his heel.

"You probably just stood on something when you walked from your bed to the door," said Mrs Jones. "I'm not at all surprised, given the amount of junk that's on your floor. I keep telling you to tidy things away, but you never listen. Stay there and I'll get you a plaster."

Alfie, however, knew that he hadn't

accidentally trodden on anything in his room.

The injury to his foot had been caused by a twig.

Chapter five

The Kingsway Colts had never won a
match against Danehill United.

They'd played them on three previous
occasions and while Danehill were far
from the best team that the Colts had
ever come up against, for some reason,
they just couldn't seem to get the better
of them.

In their home match against Danehill
earlier that season, the Colts had stormed
into an early two-goal lead courtesy of
strikes from Liam and Hayden.

However, a lucky deflected goal and an
uncharacteristic error from the team's
best defender, Danny Foreman, had
allowed their opponents to snatch an
undeserved draw after Kingsway had

controlled most of the match and missed a whole host of chances.

"Don't worry about what's happened in past games against this team," said the Colts' coach, Jimmy Grimshaw, as he delivered his pre-match team-talk. "Just concentrate on today's game. If you play as a team and work hard for each other, then you know you're good enough to beat anyone, no matter who they are. But whatever happens, win, lose or draw, the most important thing is to go out there, do your best and enjoy it."

All of the Colts' players exchanged knowing smirks. Every single one of Jimmy's team talks finished with those two words and his catchphrase had now become something of a running joke between members of the Kingsway squad.

But when Jimmy told his players to 'enjoy it' he meant it wholeheartedly. The elderly coach really did place the children's enjoyment ahead of winning football matches and although he obviously liked to see his team win, he took even greater pleasure from watching his charges play good football with smiles on their faces.

Alfie was pleased to have been picked to play in his favourite position, left midfield, for the third week running. While Jimmy firmly believed in rotating the positions of his players so that all of the children got used to playing everywhere on the pitch – including, occasionally, in goal – he had started to give some of his players more settled positions.

Pranav Jamal played in goal almost every week, Danny was more often than not in defence, Billy was usually right midfield and Liam was always up front – whether he was picked to play there or not! Chloe, Hayden and the three other Colts' squad members – Des Grey, Luke Stanford and Ollie Sudbury – still tended to play in different positions each week, but they didn't mind. Hayden was so good that it didn't really matter where he played; he was still usually voted player of the match by his teammates at the end of every game.

While the previous night's bizarre goings-on had left Alfie feeling slightly weary, and the sole of his right foot felt a bit sore due to the injury he had picked up during the strange proceedings, he was still fully focussed on the game ahead. In Mr Morris's car on the way to the game he'd been thinking about the kind of runs that Hugo Becker had been making during the previous day's Kingsway United match – both with and without the ball. Alfie was determined to emulate some of his hero's silky skills at Danehill's expense.

He didn't have to wait too long for his first chance to shine. From the kick off, Hayden and Liam worked the ball out wide to Alfie, who immediately found himself one-on-one against a Danehill defender. Without even taking a touch to control the ball, he instinctively flicked it through the defender's legs and sprinted past his flat-footed opponent to retrieve it. For a moment, Alfie worried that he'd put too much power on the ball and that it would run harmlessly out of play for a goal-kick. Fortunately, though, it had rained a lot during the previous week and the ball held up on the heavy pitch, allowing him to catch up with it just before it rolled off for a goal kick.

Alfie dragged the ball back using the bottom of his right boot and turned quickly, before crossing left footed. Although he didn't manage to get as much power into the cross as he had intended, and there was no chance of the ball reaching Liam, who Alfie had spotted was completely unmarked in the middle of the penalty area, Hayden had anticipated that the poor condition of the pitch might make it difficult for his teammate to cross the ball too far and had taken up a good position near the front post.

The ball landed right at his feet and before the Danehill goalkeeper could even shout for his defenders to mark Liam, Hayden had unselfishly rolled the ball across the goal right into the path of the striker, who was left with the simple task of blasting the ball into the net. 1-0.

It was the best possible start for the Colts. "Great cross, Alfie," shouted Hayden, as he ran to congratulate Liam.

Alfie smiled but didn't say anything. There was no way he was going to tell anybody that he had been aiming for Liam with the original cross. Not that it really mattered. The Colts were 1-0 up after less than a minute and he'd played a key role in the goal.

Alfie continued to get the better of his marker during the opening 20 minutes of the match, using a combination of skill and intelligent off-the-ball running. He couldn't believe how much he'd learned from studying Becker's movement in just one live game and couldn't help but think about how much he would improve if he could go and watch him – and the other Kingsway United players – more often.

After creating further chances for Billy and Luke, both of which were well saved by the Danehill keeper, Alfie went close to scoring himself after completely losing his marker by dropping deep and then spinning away from him just as Hayden played a clever reverse pass.

Alfie composed himself and shot hard and low across the goal, aiming for the inside side netting, just as Jimmy had so often told him to. However, he was gutted to see the ball rebound off the far post.

Then, five minutes before half-time, the Colts did get the second goal that their good play had deserved. This time it was Billy's turn to show what he could do. Although since the arrival of Hayden at the start of the season the right midfielder was no longer viewed as the Colts' star player, he was still exceptionally talented. After using his electrifying pace to beat three players, he left the Danehill goalkeeper with no chance, unleashing a cracking shot from the edge of the area which rifled into the top corner of the goal.

The Colts were in complete control of the match and while Alfie was thoroughly enjoying himself, it was becoming harder for him to hide the fact that his right foot was causing him some considerable discomfort. During the last five minutes of the first half he had started to limp heavily, and try as he might to hide the fact he was limping, there was no fooling Jimmy. He'd been a coach way too long to not know when one of his players was hurt.

At half-time the coach had little hesitation in substituting Alfie for Chloe, and while the young boy pleaded with his coach to be allowed to stay on, deep down he knew that Jimmy was right to take him off.

After finally accepting that he would be going off, Alfie sat down and removed his right boot and sock so that he could examine the sole of his injured foot. Even though the plaster that his Mum had stuck on earlier that morning was still in place, he could see that the wound had started to bleed again.

"That looks painful," said Jimmy, as Alfie quickly whipped the plaster off his foot, revealing a far nastier-looking cut than had been there prior to kick-off. "You should have told me before the game that you were hurt," admonished the elderly coach. "You've probably made it a lot worse now. How did you do it anyway?"

Alfie shrugged his shoulders. "I think I stood on a toy during the night," he said, unconvincingly.

"Must have been a sharp toy to do that much damage," replied the coach, bending down to take a closer look at the injury. "I'll just go and get some water and a plaster from the first-aid kit. We'll have it cleaned up in no time."

While Jimmy wandered off in search of the necessary supplies, the Colts' other two subs, Des and Ollie, approached their friend.

"Hey, Alfie, do you want to come and play in those trees over there with us?" asked Des, pointing in the direction of the wood which surrounded Danehill's ground.

"Maybe in a minute," replied Alfie. "I'm just going to wait for Jimmy to put a plaster on my foot. Shouldn't you two wait here, though? You'll be on in a minute. Jimmy always makes substitutions just after half-time."

"He'll call if he needs us," said Ollie,

who had only recently joined the Colts from Ashgate Athletic. Although Ollie was friendly enough, most of the Colts players were unsure as to whether Ollie really liked football that much. He always seemed more interested in playing about on the side of the pitch then he did actually chasing a ball on it. He didn't even support a team.

"I might catch up with you in a bit," said Alfie, although if he was being totally honest he was more interested in watching the rest of the game than he was in climbing trees.

Ollie and Des charged off in the direction of the wood. Alfie was a little bit surprised that Des wasn't nagging Jimmy to get onto the pitch. Unlike Ollie, Des was quite a good player, and Alfie knew that he liked football, although ever since he'd hurt his ankle the season before he had seemed to become less bothered about playing all the time.

Jimmy soon returned with some water and a plaster and began tending to Alfie's wound. "Where have Des and Ollie gone now?" the coach asked, sounding a tad exasperated. "I was just about to bring them on."

"Over there," said Alfie, gesturing in the

general direction of the trees. "I'll go over and get them if you want?"

Jimmy thought about it for a moment. "Okay, but don't rush about too much. It's probably best if you don't put too much pressure on your foot. I don't want it to start bleeding again."

Alfie agreed to be careful and then headed off in the direction of the wood.

"Ollie! Des!" he called out at the top of his voice as he approached the trees. There was no reply.

"Stop mucking about you two. Jimmy wants you." Again there was no reply.

Letting out a deep, long sigh, Alfie decided to have a quick look in the woods to see if he could see them. 'If I can't see them straight away then I'm going back,' he promised himself, silently. 'It's their fault if they miss out on a chance to play.'

However, the very second he set foot on the path leading into the wood, a shiver ran down his spine.

Alfie had seen this wood before.

Chapter six

The longer Alfie stood staring at the surrounding trees and foliage, the more he became convinced that this was the exact same wood he had encountered on the landing outside his bedroom door during the previous night.

He reached out to touch the tree closest to him. Sure enough, the bark was wet, just as it had been when he'd attempted to turn the hallway light on during the night, only to instead find himself tapping at a tree.

Alfie slowly edged further into the wood. He could not see – or hear – Des or Ollie anywhere, but he could just about make out the sound of running water above the constant tweets of the chirping birds.

An abrupt movement in some nearby bushes caught Alfie's attention. Seconds later a squirrel leapt out of the shrubbery and scampered off down the path.

Alfie pinched his right arm twice – gently at first and then much more vigorously. He knew he couldn't have been dreaming but he could not begin to make any sense out of anything that was happening. He was truly terrified.

Once more he called out for Des and Ollie, desperately hoping his teammates would be close by. Once more, though, no reply was forthcoming.

He turned around and started to make his way out of the wood as quickly as his injured foot would allow him to. Jimmy would have to go and find the two boys by himself, if indeed they hadn't already made their way back to the pitch. Alfie no longer wanted to be anywhere near the strange woods.

It should have taken less than a minute for him to find his way out of the trees. He hadn't ventured that far into them – he hadn't needed to in order to realise that this was the very wood he'd encountered in his upstairs hallway during the night. However, just as he thought he must be coming towards the edge of the wood something scuttled in front of him. Another squirrel.

Alfie watched as the squirrel ran straight past him, narrowly avoiding treading on his football boots, and then jumped into some bushes by the side of the path. He rubbed his eyes in disbelief. There could be little doubt that it was the same bush a squirrel had jumped out of previously.

'That can't be right,' Alfie thought to himself. 'I haven't once left the path so there's no way I could have gone round in a circle. It must be a different bush.'

To be certain, Alfie decided to pick up a fallen tree branch from the floor and prop it against the bush. He then continued following the path he'd been walking along just moments before.

Less than a minute later, however, he found himself standing back in the same spot. The branch propped up against the bush confirmed he had indeed walked round in a circle.

Terror now took complete hold of Alfie. He was lost. There was no way out of the wood. He tried to scream for help, but he was so scared that the words caught in his throat leaving him unable to make a sound.

Tears started to roll down his cheeks and he began to sob loudly. He tried once more to call for help, but again no sound came.

It took Alfie a good few minutes to calm himself down enough to be able to think straight. He started taking deep breaths, desperately trying to steady himself. Eventually he managed to stop himself from crying.

He'd just about managed to pull himself together when he realised that something had changed. At first he couldn't quite put his finger on just what was different but he was sure that something was.

Alfie looked around again. Everything was just as it had been moments earlier.

Then he heard something. "Great goal," someone shouted in the distance. It sounded like Luke, although Alfie couldn't be 100 per cent sure.

The fact he could hear the game was still going on calmed Alfie down even further. It was then he realised what was different. He could no longer hear the sound of birds chirping or the water flowing. The wood had fallen silent. The only noise he could hear was coming from the nearby football pitch where his friends were playing.

Without any hesitation whatsoever, Alfie started to follow the direction of the noise. Within seconds he could see the clearing through which he had originally entered the wood.

Alfie started running as fast as he could. He was so relieved to be almost out of the trees that he didn't even notice the pain in his right foot as he ran. What's more, he didn't even notice that there was someone else in the wood.

Not, that is, until he ran into her.

And that was how Alfie once again came to find himself face-to-face with Madam Zola.

Chapter seven

That Alfie found himself looking at
Madam Zola did not come as too much of
a shock to the young boy.

Ever since he had heard someone
calling his name the previous evening,
swiftly followed by the familiar tingling
of wind chimes, he'd believed it would
only be a matter of time before he met the
fortune teller again.

However, far from being pleased to see
the old woman, as he'd initially thought
he would be upon arriving home from the
Kingsway United match a day earlier,
Alfie couldn't have been any angrier.

"What do you think you're doing?" he
screeched, unable to keep the fury from
his voice.

"I think you'll find it was you who bumped into me young man," replied the fortune teller, sounding equally as angry. "You really should look where you're going. Charging around like that. You could have hurt someone. I can't believe how rude some young..."

For a moment it sounded as though the fortune teller was going to continue her rant, but all of a sudden her expression softened and a broad smile broke out on her heavily wrinkled face.

"Alfie! It is you isn't it! Oh I can't believe my eyes." All trace of the annoyance that had been present in her voice just a second earlier had now completely vanished. "I had no idea it was you. How are you? What are you doing in this wood?"

"What do you mean you had no idea it was me! Of course you knew it was me," Alfie yelled. Tears once again started to well in the corner of his eyes, and his body trembled with rage. "That's why you're here. That's why you brought me here and why you made those trees appear in my house last night. Why would you do that? Why would you try and... scare me."

Madam Zola looked bewildered. "Alfie,

why would I try and scare you? I'd never do that," she said in her most soothing voice. "I honestly have no idea what you're talking about. Brought you here...? Trees in your house...?" The fortune teller shook her head. She really did look very confused. "This all reminds me of the time you asked me about what I'd said to convince Jimmy so-and-so to return as coach of the Colts. I'd never spoken to him, or heard of him, in my life, yet you were adamant that I had. Well, I didn't have a clue what you were talking about then and I don't know now."

Alfie's anger still did not subside. "Stop playing games," he roared. "I knew I was going to see you again from the moment you called out my name when I was walking home last night. I heard wind chimes and everything. Stop pretending you didn't know you'd see me here today. You did. You know you did!"

"I honestly have no idea what you're talking about," Madam Zola answered, before chuckling loudly. "Wind chimes! That's something else you always mention when you see me. Just because I like to hang them in my tents doesn't mean that every time you hear one I'm close by."

"But every time I hear one you *are* close by," replied Alfie, the fight slowly fading out of him.

"Just coincidence then, I guess," smiled Madam Zola. "So did you enjoy the game yesterday?"

"Yeah, it was really good..." Alfie started to answer without thinking, before quickly stopping himself. "Don't try and change the subject. I still want to know what you're doing here. None of this makes any sense." He hadn't been at all surprised to hear that she'd known he'd been to watch the Kingsway United game. Somehow she always knew these kind of things about him.

The fortune teller laughed again. "Oh, you know, I'm just out and about, doing this and that. Nothing special really. Just... walking."

"You must have known I'd be playing football here, though. You know everything about me. You've told me that before."

For the slightest moment, a look of irritation flashed across Madam Zola's kindly features, but it passed so quickly that Alfie wasn't sure if he'd really seen a change in her expression or not. "Well, I must have forgotten," she replied, not entirely convincingly. "I'm a very old woman and can't always remember everything. I've told you that before, I expect, as well."

Alfie shook his head, sadly. He liked the fortune teller. He liked her a lot. And he really wanted to believe her when she said that the strange events that had occurred in the past few hours had nothing to do with her. But he just couldn't. He was convinced that, somehow, she had lured him into this wood so she could speak to him. He just didn't know how. Or why.

"Well, anyway," continued Madam Zola after a short pause. "I really must be going. I can't just stand around here all day talking to you. I have other places I need to be." The elderly fortune teller glanced down at her wrist. As ever she wasn't wearing a watch but such things didn't seem to matter to Madam Zola.

"So there really is nothing you want to tell me?" Alfie asked. "Nothing about Jasper? About why and how he's been picked for the Kingsway United Academy?"

Madam Zola shook her head. "Nope. I'm afraid I don't know anything about that."

Alfie was now feeling extremely

57

confused. Why would she have arranged to meet him if she really didn't have anything useful to tell him? Maybe she was telling the truth and their meeting had indeed just been down to pure chance.

He was on the verge of apologising to his mysterious friend when she started speaking again.

"Oh, I almost forgot to ask. Have you heard of someone called Lenny Fisher?"

Alfie thought for a moment and then shrugged his shoulders. "I don't think so. Why?"

"I found a business card earlier while I was walking in the woods. It had that man's name on it and a strange logo which I thought looked a bit like a football team's badge. I wondered if he was a famous footballer." She held the card out to the young boy and he took it from her.

Alfie looked at the card. He didn't recognise the logo but had to admit that it did indeed look like it belonged to a football team. The main picture was of an aeroplane flying over a ball, and when the young boy looked closer he saw there was also something that looked like a football on the plane's tail fin.

Underneath Lenny Fisher's name, Alfie could just about make out the faint outline of more writing. However, where the card had been lying on the wet, dirty ground for goodness knows how long prior to being picked up by Madam Zola, that part of it had become too soggy and grubby for him to be able to read what it said. Rubbing at the dirt with his fingers only made things worse and ended for good any slight hope he, or anyone else for that matter, would have of being able to decipher the words.

"Nope. I've never heard of him," he said after completing his examination of the card. "I don't recognise the badge either –

if it even is a football team's badge."

"Oh well, just thought I'd ask. Anyway, I really must be going now. Hopefully I'll see you again soon, Alfie."

The fortune teller turned and headed towards the wood's exit.

"Madam Zola," Alfie called out, just before she reached the edge of the wood.

The fortune teller turned back around.

"I'm... sorry, for yelling earlier... I guess I was just scared," he shouted.

"That's okay," Madam Zola called back, before smiling her warmest smile – the one where her brown eyes twinkled like the stars.

And with that she turned, left the wood and within moments was out of sight.

Alfie took one more look at the card that Madam Zola had given him and was just about to throw it into the trees when something stopped him from doing so.

He couldn't have explained why, but suddenly he was convinced that this card was important.

This was the real reason Madam Zola had wanted to see him.

Chapter eight

It took until the following Wednesday for
Alfie to discover that the logo on the card
given to him by Madam Zola did indeed
belong to a football club.

Finding this out, though, had not been
easy and he still hadn't managed to find
out who Lenny Fisher was.

Once he had finally navigated his way
out of the wood and back to the football
pitch, Alfie had asked Jimmy if he
recognised either the logo or the name
Lenny Fisher. Although the old man was
adamant he had seen the logo somewhere
before and was fairly sure that it was
a football team's badge, he couldn't for
the life of him think of which team it
belonged to.

Likewise, he was pretty sure he'd heard the name Lenny Fisher before as well, but again the coach couldn't quite place who he was or why he may have heard of him.

Once the game finished – the Colts had ended up winning 4-0, with Billy and Liam (again) adding to the team's two first half strikes – he'd asked his friends if they recognised the name or logo on the card. None of them did.

When he arrived home later that afternoon, Alfie spent hours flicking through some of the football yearbooks he owned, hoping to spot the unknown badge. The yearbooks included information on every single team in the professional English and Scottish leagues, as well as some non-league sides, and displayed an image of each team's badge.

This proved to be a waste of time. The badge didn't belong to any of the teams covered in any of the books.

On Monday, Alfie took the card with him to school, hoping that one of the teachers, or one of his non-Kingsway Colts playing classmates, would be able to identify the logo or maybe know who Lenny Fisher was.

None of them could help either.

One of the only people who Alfie didn't bother to ask was Jasper. If Jimmy, the teachers and some of the finest minds in school couldn't identify the badge, then Alfie figured that the chances of Jasper being able to help lay somewhere between slim and none.

What's more, Alfie guessed that even in the highly unlikely event that Jasper did know something, he probably wouldn't tell him anyway, so asking would just be pointless.

By Tuesday, Alfie had decided that if the logo really was a football team's crest, then it must belong to a foreign football team. Just why Madam Zola would have given him a card belonging to a team from overseas, Alfie couldn't even begin to guess – but then he was fully used to the fortune teller's cryptic ways by now.

However, after yet more wasted hours searching for the logo – this time conducted using the Internet on his Mum and Dad's computer – he was still no closer to finding out anything useful.

As is so often the case, the answer to Alfie's question finally came when he wasn't actually looking for it. He had all but given up hope of finding out anything useful about the card and had barely given it a moment's thought during school on Wednesday.

In fact, by the end of school that day his mind was only on one thing – *Kick Off* magazine.

Although Alfie generally detested reading, he made exceptions when it came to football magazines and *Kick Off* was his absolute favourite. Every Wednesday after school, Alfie went with his Mum and Megan to their local newsagents to pick up the latest copy of the mag, which was reserved for him by Sammy Reeves, the shopkeeper.

Today was no different.

Alfie rushed into the shop, hurriedly yanking at the money in his pocket which had been given to him by his Mum only a few minutes earlier.

Unfortunately – or fortunately as it turned out – Alfie had a habit of cramming items picked up at various intervals during the day into his pockets, and by the time he finally managed to wrestle the three £1 coins out of his overflowing pocket, he'd also managed to deposit a number of half-used tissues, two pencils, a pen, a blob of blu-tack, a button, a piece of lego and the card belonging to Lenny Fisher, over Sammy's counter.

Sheepishly, Alfie began to gather up all the unwanted items when Sammy suddenly stopped him.

"Where did you get that from?" asked Sammy, an elderly man who had owned the newsagents for as long as either of Alfie's parents could remember.

It took Alfie a moment to realise what Sammy was talking about, but then he noticed that the shopkeeper was looking pointedly at the card.

"This? Oh, I found it in the wood by Danehill Park over the weekend," he answered, almost honestly.

"Well, well, well. I haven't seen that badge for many, many years. Not since I was probably just a bit older than you, in fact."

Alfie's face suddenly lit up. "You've seen this badge before?" he exclaimed excitedly. "Is it a football team's badge?"

"It is indeed," said Sammy, taking the card from Alfie and examining it closely. A smile spread across the old shop keeper's face as he fixed his gaze on the logo. "Or at least it was. It belonged to a football team called Kingsway Harriers. Ever heard of them before?"

Alfie shook his head, his eyes fixed firmly on Sammy's face.

"Didn't think you would have," the old man continued, still smiling and looking at the card. "Kingsway Harriers used to be a professional team back when I was a young lad. They were even bigger than Kingsway United back then – already a professional team when United got accepted into the league. I had some good times watching the Harriers play. Good times indeed."

"What happened to them?"

Sammy looked thoughtful for a moment and then took his eyes off the card and directed them at Alfie instead.

"Harriers never really had a lot of money," he said, sadly. "Even back in the days when money wasn't that important in football you still needed a little bit in order to survive. As soon as Kingsway United got promoted it split the town's fan base in two and most fans eventually drifted towards United. They had just been taken over by a rich local businessman, had a brand new stadium and most fans thought they had the better prospects for success. A few years later Harriers got relegated from the football league and a couple of seasons after that they... Well, they ceased to exist."

Alfie listened to Sammy's tale in rapt silence, soaking in all that the old man had to say. He loved listening to older people talk about football's 'good old days'.

"All a long time ago now," the shopkeeper sighed, wistfully.

Sammy continued to reminisce further for a couple more minutes, but by then Alfie's thoughts were starting to turn to other questions.

"So, if Kingsway Harriers aren't a real team anymore, how come I found this card?" he asked as soon as Sammy had finished speaking. "It doesn't look that old."

"Well," answered Sammy after a short pause. "Rumour has it that a new Harriers team is forming. Just a local league team at the moment, but apparently they've got big plans to reach the professional leagues again one day. To be honest, I've heard several rumours over the years that the Harriers would reform, but nothing has ever come of them. Still, looks like maybe something will happen this time," he added, nodding towards the card he held in his hand.

"Do you know who Lenny Fisher is?" asked Alfie.

"Fisher," repeated Sammy. "Lenny Fisher? The name does ring a bell, but I can't think why. I'll have a think over the next week and if I come up with anything I'll let you know next Wednesday."

Alfie thanked the shopkeeper for his help, paid for his magazine, took the card back off Sammy, and left the shop to rejoin his Mum and sister on the pavement outside.

He finally knew who the logo belonged to. Now all he had to do now was find out who Lenny Fisher was and try to discover exactly why Madam Zola had given him the card in the first place.

Chapter nine

"Ah yes, the Kingsway Harriers," said Jimmy Grimshaw. "So that's who the badge belonged to? I knew I recognised it from somewhere..."

It was Saturday morning and for the players of the Kingsway Colts that meant only one thing – training.

Alfie had rushed over to tell Jimmy of his discovery regarding the card's logo as soon as Mr Morris had dropped him and Billy off at the Kingsway Recreation Ground.

"... I'm a couple of years younger than Sammy Reeves so I never actually got to see Kingsway Harriers play myself," the elderly coach continued. "I've always been a huge Kingsway United fan, but I do just about remember the Harriers when they were a league team. I recall that quite a few people were upset when the team folded and many blamed United for stealing their fans."

"Do you know anything about them possibly becoming a team again?" Alfie asked. He was desperate to find out as much as he could about the Harriers. He knew that Madam Zola must have given him the card for a reason, and he figured it had something to do with the news Sammy had told him regarding the Harriers' plans to once again become a professional football team.

"Just the rumours that everyone else has read about in the local papers," answered Jimmy. "Apparently, a new Harriers team is going to start playing in the local leagues next season, but the potential owners have got big plans and quite a bit of money behind them and are hoping to one day become a professional team again. That Lenny Fisher has probably got something to do with them reforming. Maybe his name's been in the papers and that's why I thought I'd heard of him when you asked me last week."

Alfie nodded. That made sense, but it still didn't give him any clues as to why the name Lenny Fisher was printed on the card Madam Zola had given him.

"Anyway, that's enough chit-chat for now," said Jimmy, clapping his hands together enthusiastically. "It's time to start the session. We've got a tough game against Rickton Rovers tomorrow – we need to make sure we're as ready as we can possibly be if we're going to give them a good game."

Alfie had spent so much of the past week pre-occupied with trying to figure out, firstly who the badge on the card belonged to and later why Madam Zola had given him a card with a long-extinct football team's crest on it, that he'd hardly spent any time at all thinking about the Colts' upcoming game against Rickton.

Alfie tried to force the mystery of the card to the back of his mind in order to concentrate fully on the following day's game.

Jimmy was right. The Rickton game would be tough.

Very tough indeed.

The Colts had only ever played them once before; at a tournament during the previous summer. While they had drawn that match 1-1, Kingsway had been largely outplayed and Rickton had gone on to win the whole tournament, ultimately beating Keith Johnson's North Malling Town team in the final.

During training it was obvious for all to see that every single Colts player knew they would have to be at their best the following day if they were going to give Rickton Rovers a competitive game. Their behaviour throughout the entire session was impeccable, even during the dribbling drill which Jimmy quite often liked getting his players to do.

The drill involved the children moving quickly in and out of cones spread around a small grid, using different parts of their feet to keep the ball under control. Usually, when Jimmy set this drill up, a number of players would moan, stating that the exercise was boring – particularly Liam, who only ever wanted to do drills which involved shooting, and Ollie, who never really looked that enthused about anything as far as football was concerned.

Today, however, Jimmy couldn't have wished for his charges to apply themselves to the task any better, and as a reward for their positive attitude he'd allowed them to have a slightly longer match than usual at the end of the session.

As ever, Alfie, Billy and Hayden tried to convince Jimmy to let them go on the same team for the match but, as ever, Jimmy refused.

The coach always tried to make sure that Billy and Hayden played on separate teams during training matches. They were by far the Colts' two best players and, although Jimmy would never admit it out loud, it would leave the other team at a severe disadvantage to be up against those two boys.

Hayden had once complained to Jimmy that he was never allowed to go on the same team as Billy, but the coach had just laughed off the protest and said that Hayden was exaggerating.

He would never dream of telling any of the squad his real reasons for attempting to keep the two apart.

While all the Colts' players themselves fully realised that Billy and Hayden were by far the team's two best players, Jimmy was always very careful to tell his players that they were as good as each other, not wanting to single anyone out for individual praise at the expense of others.

Yet, as Jimmy stood to the side of the

cone-marked pitch, watching the children play their match, he had to admit that each and every week Billy and Hayden were getting better and better.

Both boys not only had great ball skills, but they were also very good readers of the game, hard workers and, most importantly in his opinion, not at all big-headed about their obvious talents – especially Hayden, who didn't seem to have any indication of how good he actually was.

During the previous week's game, Jimmy had heard a few of the players and parents discussing how strange it was that Hayden and Billy hadn't been offered trials for the Kingsway United Elite Centre when Jasper had been picked for the Academy.

This is something that the elderly coach had himself been wondering about for some time. Although Jimmy wasn't one for sticking his nose in, he'd been a youth football coach for a long, long time and couldn't remember seeing too many players as good as either Hayden or Billy.

As he watched Billy expertly make his way past three attempted tackles before delivering an inch-perfect cross towards Chloe's head, Jimmy decided it was time to be a little more pro-active as far as his team were concerned. He'd noticed on countless occasions throughout the season that an Elite Centre scout had been present at North Malling Town's games; no doubt a result of constant nagging from Keith Johnson.

So right there and then Jimmy resolved to phone the Elite Centre that afternoon to try and get a scout down to watch the Colts' match against Rickton the following day.

It was time to give his players a chance to show off their skills.

Chapter ten

It had started raining at almost the exact moment the cars belonging to the Kingsway Colts' parents began arriving at the Kingsway Recreation Ground.

Starting out as a light drizzle, the rain became progressively heavier as the players carried out their warm up exercises – which mostly consisted of shooting multiple balls at a helpless Pranav in goal – and as kick-off approached it was, in the words of Mr Morris, "absolutely bucketing down."

As Jimmy called his players over to give them their pre-match team talk, it was obvious to Alfie that the coach was not his usual jovial self. Jimmy spent so much of his time being smiley and cheery that it was really noticeable when he wasn't in the greatest of moods. This was definitely one of those rare days.

He simply looked miserable and fed up. 'Must be the weather,' Alfie decided to himself.

The elderly coach forced a weak smile as the children all ran over to listen to what he had to say. "Okay, we know that this lot are good, so just go out there and do your best."

A look of confusion swept over the faces of the Kingsway players as they waited for their coach to say more. Jimmy usually rambled on for a good few minutes in his team-talks, but it soon became apparent that he had nothing more to add to this particular talk. He hadn't even told them to enjoy the game – and he *always* did that!

"What are you waiting for?" Jimmy asked, trying, but not quite managing, to stop himself from sounding too grumpy. "Go and get in your positions."

For a while none of the Kingsway players said anything. They were all a little baffled by Jimmy's abrupt team talk and were each wondering what they had done wrong to put their coach in such a surly mood. Eventually Chloe broke the silence. "Well, it would be useful to... erm... know what the team is."

Jimmy looked sternly at Chloe. For the slightest moment she thought he was going to yell at her, but then a broad smile cracked out across his face and he once again resembled the Jimmy the children knew and admired.

"Yes. That would be quite a useful thing to know wouldn't it?" Jimmy said, before chuckling heartily. "I'm sorry kids. I'm not feeling quite myself this morning. I think the weather must be getting to me." Alfie smiled to himself, pleased to have his own diagnosis for Jimmy's bad mood confirmed. "The team to start will be Pranav in goal, Des and Chloe in defence, Alfie on the left of midfield, Billy on the right and Hayden in the middle, with Liam up front. Ollie, Danny and Luke will start on the side but you'll definitely get on, either at half-time or just after."

The players rushed off to take their positions, while Luke, Danny and Ollie grabbed a ball and started to kick it to each other, leaving Jimmy standing all alone by the side of the pitch.

While it was true that Jimmy didn't particularly like the rain, his dour mood that morning had nothing whatsoever to do with the rotten weather. Instead it was the telephone conversation that he'd had with a man at the Elite Centre the previous afternoon which was the real cause of his low spirits.

Initially, when Jimmy had mentioned that he was the coach of an under 10s football team and said that there were a couple of players who he'd like to recommend to be watched, the man at the other end of the line had seemed friendly and helpful.

However, as soon as Jimmy mentioned that the team he coached was the Kingsway Colts, the attitude of the man to whom he was speaking changed.

Almost immediately the man started to sound disinterested and whereas just moments before he'd said he would do all he could to get a scout down to watch the players being recommended to him, he now started to make excuses.

Suddenly Jimmy was told that all the scouts were already assigned to games and that it was very unlikely they'd be able to get anyone to go and watch the team for a good few weeks.

While Jimmy knew that getting a scout down to watch that day's game had been a long-shot at such short notice, he had been left seething by the attitude of the man on the phone who couldn't have made it any plainer to Jimmy that the Elite Centre were not interested in his recommendations.

Although he couldn't be 100 per cent sure as to why the man on the phone had quickly become so disinterested once he'd learned that he represented the Kingsway Colts, Jimmy was fairly certain that Keith was involved somehow. Why else would a scout be present at so many North Malling games unless Keith had some kind of influence at the Elite Centre? It would certainly explain Jasper's swift rise to the Elite Centre and beyond.

This feeling of suspicion had been strengthened just moments before Jimmy had given his brisk team-talk. Upon getting out of his car and walking to the Colts' home pitch, the coach had walked past another of the Kingsway Recreation Ground pitches where North Malling Town happened to be playing. And, sure enough, there was Keith, deep in conversation with a man wearing a Kingsway United training kit.

Although Jimmy didn't recognise the man, and couldn't remember seeing him before, the old man was certain that he must be a scout.

What Jimmy couldn't have known, however, was that the man Keith was speaking to was the exact same man he'd spoken to on the phone a day earlier.

Not only that, it was also the same man that Alfie had seen Keith talking to just over a week ago at the Kingsway United match.

Chapter eleven

There could be little doubt that Rickton
Rovers were the best team the Kingsway
Colts had ever played. Although they
didn't necessarily have any individuals
that were any better, or even as good,
as either Hayden or Billy, the way they
played together as a team was highly
impressive.

Jimmy had always encouraged the Colts
to play good passing football, but they
simply couldn't rival Rickton's non-stop,
slick passing and clever movement. It
was as if the opposition had two extra
players on the pitch... there was always
someone unmarked and available to be
passed to.

Alfie and his teammates had spent the

opening ten minutes of the match doing little more than chasing shadows as the Rickton players simply passed the ball around them.

None of their players ever seemed to take more than three touches of the ball once they were in possession of it. On the few occasions that the Colts had managed to get hold of the ball they found themselves closed down so quickly that they didn't have any time to think about what they then wanted to do with it.

However, due to a combination of dogged defending and a seeming reluctance from the Rovers' attackers to shoot when well placed, the Colts' had somehow made it to the ten-minute mark still on level terms. And, as the rain continued to hammer down, Rickton were starting to find it increasingly difficult to play their quick, short passing game.

The pitch was cutting up and becoming ever stickier and passes that had been skimming across the wet surface only a few minutes earlier were now starting to get stuck in the churned-up, sludgy mud.

Rovers, though, were determined to persevere with their sleek playing style in spite of the conditions. However, with their passes starting to go astray, the Colts were beginning to see more and more of the ball and as half-time approached they were growing in confidence, sensing collectively that they had a chance to snatch a win against a far superior team.

Just before the interval, Alfie managed to intercept a pass from a Rickton defender which had been intended for the right midfielder. The defender was now badly out of position and Alfie looked up to see that Liam was standing in plenty of space near the edge of the opposition penalty area.

Although Jimmy was normally insistent that his team should try and keep the ball on the ground at all times, Alfie realised that it was Rickton's refusal to abandon their fluent passing style that had allowed Kingsway to come more into the game.

Alfie used the bottom of his right foot to roll the ball slightly in front of him and then, with his left foot, he scooped the ball high into the air aiming to find the unmarked Liam.

Although the pass wasn't 100 per cent accurate, Liam was standing in so much space that it didn't have to be. The Colts' striker easily got to the ball ahead of the recovering Rovers' defender and, out of nowhere, he was through on goal.

Having been impressed with Alfie's improvised pass to present him with the opportunity, Liam decided he would try something similar. As the Rickton goalkeeper rushed out of his goal to narrow the shooting angle, Liam dug his foot under the ball and quickly lifted his leg, attempting an audacious chip over the head of the advancing 'keeper.

The Rickton number one could only watch in horror as the ball sailed over his head. Unfortunately for Liam, though, he had got just too much lift on the ball and it agonisingly cleared the crossbar by mere inches.

There was barely enough time for the goalkeeper to restart the game before the ref blew his whistle for half-time.

"Unlucky Liam, that was a great effort," said Alfie, as the players made their way towards their respective coaches.

"Cheers, Alf. It was a great pass too. I probably wouldn't have thought to try that otherwise."

Billy jogged over to catch up with his two friends. "Wow, they're good!" he said, breathlessly. "I don't think I've ever had to do so much running in one half."

Liam and Alfie nodded their agreement. All six of the Colts' outfield players looked thoroughly puffed-out from their defensive efforts and, although they would never admit it, none of them would have been too cross if Jimmy decided to take them off at half-time.

As the three friends neared Jimmy and the rest of their teammates, their attention was suddenly taken by a boy on the sideline.

The boy was standing by himself, doing keepy-ups. Alfie had never seen someone so skilful in all his life. The boy was using every body part imaginable to keep the ball off the floor. It seemed to take an age before he finally lost control of the ball and that was only when trying to catch it on the back of his neck.

"That was amazing," gasped Billy.

"I could do that," lied Liam, prompting Alfie and Billy to look at each other and roll their eyes.

"He looks familiar," said Alfie, looking fixedly at the boy who had resumed his ball juggling tricks.

"His name's Reuben Ryan," said a voice from behind them. It was the Rickton goalkeeper who was himself still making his way off the pitch. "He used to play for

86

us last season, but he's not allowed to any more as he plays for the Kingsway United Academy."

"That's it," Alfie exclaimed excitedly, snapping his fingers. "He's the boy that was on the pitch at the United game last week. You know, one of the only Academy players that looked like he was actually any good."

Although Billy and Liam hadn't recognised him at first, now Alfie pointed out who it was they could clearly recall the first boy who they'd seen have a shot – the one that had curled the ball expertly into the top left corner of the goal.

"He's better than good, he's class," confirmed the Rovers' goalkeeper, before jogging off to join his own teammates for their half-time talk.

Alfie, Billy and Liam had all but reached Jimmy and the rest of their friends when Alfie suddenly had a thought.

"I'll be right back. There's something that I need to ask that boy," he said, gesturing towards Reuben.

"Alf, what are you doing?" Billy called after him, but it was too late. Alfie was already sprinting off in the direction of the 'keepy-up king'.

Alfie watched silently in awe as Reuben carried on executing his latest round of tricks and skills – even the flashiest of performing seals would be jealous at what he could do with a ball.

After a short while the boy noticed Alfie staring gog-eyed at him and let the ball fall to the ground. "Can I help you?" he asked, a hint of suspicion clearly audible in his voice.

"Erm," began Alfie. "I know this sounds a bit weird, but I've got to ask you... you were at the Kingsway United match last week weren't you? Shooting at goal during half-time. I was there and I'm sure I recognise you."

"That's right." Reuben tried not to smile, but couldn't help himself. He quite liked the feeling of being recognised. "Is that all you wanted to know?"

"Not quite," continued Alfie, awkwardly. "It's just that... I don't know how to put this... but... well, I sort of know one of the other boys in the Academy and to be honest, I think he's... well... a little bit rubbish." Alfie knew he was being slightly harsh. Jasper wasn't that bad, but he was clearly nowhere near good enough to be in the Academy either.

"Jasper Johnson by any chance?" replied Reuben, taking Alfie completely by surprise.

"Yes," responded Alfie immediately. "How did you know?"

"Lucky guess." Reuben smiled again. "Yeah, I don't think he's any good either. He thinks he is, though. The way he carries on you'd think he was already a professional."

Now it was Alfie's turn to smile. That sure sounded like Jasper.

"It's not just Jasper, though. It's weird," continued Reuben. "I don't think that many of the players there are that good. Most of the players playing here today are better than half of the players in the Academy."

Although Reuben didn't give any indication as to whether he included Alfie in this, Alfie was only too happy to believe that he did.

"Why do you think that is?" Alfie asked.

Reuben shrugged his shoulders. "No Idea. Tommy Fisher must rate them, I suppose."

Alfie's ears suddenly pricked up. "Tommy Fisher," he repeated. "Are you sure you don't mean Lenny Fisher."

Reuben shot Alfie a quizzical look. He was starting to lose patience with this skinny boy who he'd never met before. "No. It's definitely Tommy Fisher," he said sharply. "He's the head of the Kingsway United Elite Centre and Academy for the under 10s. I've no idea who Lenny Fisher is. Anyway shouldn't you be going? I think your team are waiting for you."

Alfie glanced behind him to see that Jimmy and all his friends were all staring in his direction, clearly getting fed up with waiting for him. He thanked Reuben for his time and then jogged back over to join the rest of the Kingsway squad.

He smiled at the sarcastic cheers that greeted his arrival, and after Jimmy had checked to make sure Alfie was okay, he began his much delayed team-talk. However, although Alfie tried his best to concentrate, much of what his coach had to say went in one ear and straight out of the other. His thoughts were elsewhere.

Tommy Fisher and Lenny Fisher – surely they had to be connected somehow. Didn't they?

Chapter twelve

By the time the referee blew his whistle to bring the match to a, slightly earlier than expected, end, the game was being played in near farcical conditions.

The rain had continued to fall and, if anything, had actually got heavier as the match progressed. This had left the pitch looking more like something you would find in a pig-sty at the local farm than something meant for playing football on.

The outcome being that both Kingsway and Rickton had struggled to get any kind of rhythm going in the second half and as the match neared its conclusion, and the players became increasingly wet, cold and fed up, both teams were happy to settle for a 0-0 draw.

As the players from both sides sprinted as fast as their tired legs would allow them in the direction of the car park, desperate to get into their parents' warm cars, Alfie noticed that the North Malling Town game was still going on. The players on both sides looked as miserable as those involved in the game he'd been playing in; yet Alfie knew there was no way that Keith would ever let a match finish early – especially if his team weren't winning.

All of the parents watching that game had already retreated to the comfort of their cars and Alfie could see them vigorously wiping at their steamed-up windscreens in an attempt to get as good a view possible of the remaining few minutes of the match. The only people still standing on the sidelines were the opposition team's coach – who looked as despondent as the players – Keith, who didn't even seem to be aware that it was raining and, standing right beside him, another man who was wearing a Kingsway United tracksuit.

Alfie slowed his run as he neared Keith. From a distance he thought he'd recognised the third man, but couldn't remember where from. As he got closer, though, he quickly placed exactly who it was. It was the man that he'd seen Keith talking to at the Kingsway United match.

"What are you gawping at, Jones?" yelled Keith, having caught Alfie staring in his direction.

Alfie didn't respond. He just put his head down, picked up his pace, and sprinted towards the sanctuary of Billy's Dad's car.

On the drive back to his house, Alfie hardly said a word to either Billy or Mr Morris. Billy hadn't seen his friend so quiet in ages – probably not since he'd cried in the car following a match against Deansview Juniors around 14 months earlier. On that occasion, Alfie's distress had been caused by constant taunting from Jasper and unfair treatment from Keith, who was then the Colts' coach. While Billy was almost certain that bullying was not the cause of his best buddy's solemn mood on this occasion, he couldn't help but feel a little concerned.

"You okay, Alf?" he asked, after a few minutes of watching his friend staring absent-mindedly out of the window.

There was no response.

"Alfie," tried Billy again, a little louder this time. "You okay?"

Once again no response was forthcoming. Alfie didn't even show any signs that he'd heard Billy speak.

Finally losing patience with being ignored, Billy gently jabbed a finger into Alfie's ribs, causing his friend to yelp in shock.

"Owww! What did you do that for?"

Billy laughed. "I've just asked you a question twice, but you didn't seem to hear me. Had to get your attention somehow, didn't I? You alright?"

"Sorry," replied Alfie, turning a little red. "I've just been thinking that's all."

"That sounds dangerous," chuckled Mr Morris. He liked to think of himself as being a bit of a comedian. "Have you got a headache now?"

"Ha ha, very funny," said Alfie, in a tone designed to make it clear that his friend's Dad was being anything but. "When I was talking to that Reuben, the boy who was doing all those tricks, he said something about the Kingsway United Under 10s Academy being run by a man called Tommy Fisher."

"So what?" Billy responded, sounding confused.

"I don't know. It's just that... well... the name on that card I found was Lenny

95

Fisher. Just seems a bit strange, I guess."

"Fisher is not exactly an unusual surname, Alfie" said Mr Morris. "It's probably just a coincidence."

"Maybe," acknowledged Alfie, although he didn't think it was. That card had been given to him by Madam Zola for a reason. That he should then discover the man directly responsible for Jasper being in the Academy was also called Fisher was just too convenient to be mere coincidence.

"It's not just that, though," he continued after a brief pause. "When we were running back to the car I noticed that Keith was standing next to a man wearing a Kingsway United tracksuit. I'm pretty sure that it was the same man I saw him with at the match last week."

Billy looked at Alfie, clearly not sure what his friend was trying to get at. "And..." he said, realising his friend didn't have anything else to add.

"I don't know," admitted Alfie again. "I just think that there's something strange going on. We all know that Jasper's not good enough to be in the Academy – yet he's in it. I find a card with the name 'Lenny Fisher' written on it, and then discover that it's a man called Tommy

Fisher who runs the Under 10s Academy. Then there's the man that Keith was talking to. Why would he still be out talking to him in that weather when all the parents had even gone to sit in their cars?"

"It all sounds very mysterious, Alfie," laughed Mr Morris. "Fancy yourself as a bit of a detective do you? Or a spy even? I can see it now, the name's Jones... Alfie Jones."

Billy laughed as his Dad started doing some, frankly not very good, impressions of James Bond. Even Alfie had to smile.

However, while he may not have much fancied being a detective when he was older – he was going to be a professional football player, no matter what – this was one mystery that Alfie was determined to solve.

Chapter thirteen

He really didn't want to have to do it. He really wished there was another way.

Something.

Anything.

Yet the more he tried to think of an alternative, the more he realised there really wasn't anything else he could do. If Alfie wanted to find out the answers to all of his questions – and he did – then he was going to have to talk to Jasper.

By Monday break-time, Alfie had already planned out in his mind a hundred times just what he was going to say to his nemesis. Although he didn't expect Jasper to give him any particularly useful information, Alfie believed there was definitely one way that he could get his former teammate to speak more openly than he would usually.

He was going to have to flatter him.

The thought of having to be complimentary to Jasper caused Alfie to shudder as he strode, what he hoped passed as confidently, across the playground towards him.

Even though he could only see Jasper's back, Alfie had known it was him from right over the other side of the playground. Not only was Jasper about a head taller than most people in the school – including all of the Year 6 children and a fair few of the teachers – he was also the only person wearing a Kingsway United Academy tracksuit over his blue school jumper.

Alfie couldn't remember the last time he'd seen Jasper wearing anything other than that top. 'I bet he even sleeps in it,' Alfie thought to himself, before quickly trying to shake the image of Jasper drooling onto his pillow out of his mind.

Having arrived within touching distance of his target, Alfie stretched out his hand to tap Jasper on the shoulder.

However, before any contact could be made, Jasper spun on his heals to face Alfie. It was almost as if he had a sixth sense and had known he was being approached.

Jasper simply towered over Alfie, who was one of the smallest boys in Year 5, and while the scowl on the larger boy's face would have scared off less hardy souls, Alfie was not in the least bit intimidated. Well... maybe just a little.

"What do you want, muppet?" Jasper asked, angrily.

This was exactly the kind of greeting Alfie had expected to receive. So far so good. "I met one of your Academy teammates yesterday," he said, not even bothering to say hello to Jasper.

"And... am I supposed to care? Which one?"

"I think he said his name was Reuben."

A look of anger flashed across Jasper's face. He hated Reuben, with all his flashy ball tricks and skills. He was sure that Reuben was always trying to make him look foolish when they played against each other in practice matches – he'd been nutmegged four times by him during the last training session, much to Jasper's disgust and most of his teammates' all too obvious glee.

"So what?" Jasper replied, grumpily.

"So I was just wondering if you'd been

teaching him some skills? He was doing some tricks on the side of the pitch yesterday when we were playing Rickton and they looked just like the ones you sometimes do in the playground."

Although he was severely tempted, Alfie just about managed to stop himself from laughing. He wasn't usually that good at telling fibs – he normally gave himself away, either by bursting into a fit of giggles or by turning bright red.

Jasper scanned Alfie's face, trying to detect whether he was being mocked or not. However, in Jasper's misguided imagination, he truly believed that he really could perform keepy-ups just as

101

well as Reuben, so he was only too willing to give Alfie the benefit of the doubt; just as Alfie had thought he would.

"Well, I did teach him a few things," said Jasper, trying, and utterly failing, to sound modest.

"I thought you must have."

"Is that all you wanted to know, muppet? I've already told you that you can have my autograph whenever you want it."

Alfie laughed in what he hoped was a good humoured manner. "Who knows? Maybe one day I will be asking for your autograph. Reuben said you were probably the Academy team's best player." Alfie desperately hoped his cheeks weren't glowing as red as he feared they would be. Fortunately they weren't.

Jasper's face lit up. "Did Reuben really say that?" he asked, sounding a little bit surprised.

Alfie nodded earnestly.

Jasper took a moment to think about what he was hearing. For a moment Alfie thought that Jasper would see right through his blatant lies, but then the larger boy smiled and nodded. "Well, thinking about it, I probably am one of the star players. Actually, I am probably the best player. Tommy is always telling my Dad how good he thinks I am."

"Tommy Fisher?" Alfie enquired.

Jasper shot Alfie a quizzical glance. "That's right. How do you know who Tommy is?"

"Reuben mentioned him," said Alfie, uttering pretty much his first truthful sentence since he'd started the conversation with Jasper.

"Yeah, well, he was only telling my Dad yesterday about how he thinks my size and strength make me stand out from the rest of the team. He said he expects me to do big things in the future."

"Is that who your Dad was talking to yesterday?"

"Yeah, Tommy goes and watches a lot of North Malling games. He says that... hey, what do you want to know all this for, muppet?"

Alfie shrugged his shoulders.

"Look, just accept it, I'm going to be a star when I'm older and you'll still be what you are now... A nobody. A complete muppet. I heard about the Kingsway Colts yesterday, finishing a game early just because it was *raining*. Rubbish. You all think you're great – you, Hayden,

103

Billy, Liam... Well it's me who's in the Academy. Not any of you. Me!"

Jasper continued to mock Alfie and his friends for a good two minutes more before turning around to signal their conversation was over.

But Alfie had hardly listened to any of the last few insults that Jasper had hurled at him and his Colts' teammates. He'd already found out just what he wanted to know.

Keith was indeed friends with Tommy Fisher, and there was little doubt in Alfie's mind that this friendship was directly responsible for Jasper's selection in the Kingsway United Academy.

But what could he do about it?

Chapter fourteen

Mrs Jones always knew when Alfie wasn't feeling quite right.

There were little tell-tale signs that gave it away. Today it was the fact that they were almost halfway home from school, and he hadn't once tried to wind his younger sister up, which signalled to her that all was not as it should be.

In fact, now she came to think about it, he'd barely acknowledged either her or Megan from the moment she'd picked them up.

"You're very quiet today, darling. Is everything okay at school?" Mrs Jones asked in her typically soothing manner.

"Yep," said Alfie, without taking his eyes away from the pavement.

"I bet he's got a girlfriend," said Megan, excitedly. "It says in one of my magazines that boys go all quiet and thoughtful when they're in love," she squealed.

For a moment Alfie looked, and sounded, genuinely repulsed. "Yuck. Don't be disgusting, Megan. Course I haven't got a girlfriend. What would I want a girlfriend for? Most girls are just plain weird. Like you!"

"I bet it's Chloe. You're always talking to her at playtime." said Megan, seemingly not having heard a word of what her brother had just said. "Alfie and Chloe sitting in a tree, k i s s i n g," she began to sing.

"No it's not Chloe. She's one of my best friends. That's why I talk to her... Its not anyone... I haven't got a girlfriend... I don't want a girlfriend. Mum can you tell her to be quiet."

Mrs Jones laughed. This was more like the kind of scene she was used to during their walks home from school. "Megan, stop annoying your brother. I'm sure Alfie will tell us all about his new girlfriend when he's ready."

Alfie shot his Mum an angry look but didn't bother to say anything – he knew she was looking for a reaction. Mrs Jones

106

smiled and slapped the back of her hand theatrically, causing Megan to laugh out loud. "Seriously, though, everything is alright isn't it, darling?"

"Yes Mum, everything's fine. I've just got a lot on my mind. There are some things I need to work out. That's all."

"Anything I can help with?"

Alfie politely declined his Mum's offer. He couldn't see how she'd be able to help him learn what he needed to know.

From the moment he'd finished speaking to Jasper earlier that day, Alfie had been trying to figure out what he should do next. He simply didn't have a clue.

Okay, so he now knew that Keith did indeed know Tommy Fisher, but did that really matter? Unpleasant as Keith may be, Alfie was fairly sure there were no laws against him having friends. What's more, while he was also fairly certain that Keith's friendship with Tommy was probably the reason Jasper had been picked for the Academy, what could a ten-year-old boy do about that?

Likewise, he was also pretty sure that Tommy Fisher and Lenny Fisher must be connected in some way, but again he didn't have an inkling of how he was

107

supposed to go about finding out what their relationship was.

'Why did Madam Zola give me that card?' Alfie mused, as he meandered silently along the pavement, trying his best to ignore his sister, who was continuing to sing stupid songs about him and Chloe being in love.

He was sure that the fortune teller must have given him the card for a reason – there was always a reason behind everything that Madam Zola said and did – but more than a week had passed since he'd seen her in the woods and he felt no closer to finding out what her motive for giving him the card was.

Alfie was still deep in thought when his Mum suddenly stopped outside the newsagents owned by Sammy Reeves. "I've just got to pop in here and get some milk."

"Can I have a magazine? Or some chocolate? Please, please, pretty please." Megan asked, pleadingly.

"Maybe a magazine if you promise to be good. Would a packet of football cards put you in a better mood, darling?" she asked Alfie.

Alfie nodded enthusiastically. He loved getting packs of football cards.

"Maybe you could share them with Chloe," mocked Megan, prompting Alfie to start whining to his Mum, begging her to make his sister shut up.

Inside the shop, Sammy was pleased to see Alfie. "Hello Alfie, I'm glad you've popped in," he said. "I read an article in today's *Kingsway Courier* that may be of interest to you."

"Have United signed someone?" Alfie asked, animatedly.

"No, no. It's not actually anything about Kingsway United. It's about Kingsway Harriers. Here, take a look."

The shopkeeper held up the back page of the Kingsway area's local newspaper. Alfie immediately saw why Sammy had thought the story would be of interest to him. '**Harriers given permission to reform**' was the main headline running across the width of the page.

"They're going to be holding an open trial on Saturday afternoon at the Kingsway Recreation Ground," continued Sammy, saving Alfie the trouble of having to read the article for himself.

"They'll only be playing in the top county league next season, but apparently they have plans in place to become a professional football league team again within the next five years."

"Wow," said Alfie, sounding impressed. "It would be cool to have two proper teams in Kingsway."

"It certainly would," said Sammy, who was evidently quite excited about the prospect of getting to see the team he had supported as a young boy play once again. "But that's not all. The article also mentions Lenny Fisher. There's even a picture of him."

The young boy snatched the paper out of Sammy's hand before the shopkeeper had a chance to tell Alfie what the article said about him. He began scanning the page, desperately looking for the name, and about halfway through the article he found what he was looking for.

'The team's chairman will be Lenny Fisher, who played for the Kingsway Harriers back when they were still a professional team. Mr Fisher was delighted by the FA's decision to allow the reformed Harriers a place in the county league. "It's been a long, hard process trying to get everything in place so that we can reform the Harriers," he said. "We now have a brand new ground, a place in the league, a little bit of money behind

us... all we need is some players. After Saturday's trials I'm sure we'll have an even better idea of the quality of player we'll have available to us next season".'

"So Lenny Fisher used to play for the Harriers," stated Alfie, once he'd finished reading the article.

"Indeed he did," smiled Sammy. "That's why I thought I'd recognised his name when you asked me about him last week. Now that I've had a proper chance to think about it, I can just about remember him. He was only very young when he first got into the team, maybe 17 or 18. I'm pretty sure he only became a first team regular in the year the Harriers got relegated. Quite a promising player as I recall, although once the Harriers went out of business I never heard of him again. Well, not until now."

Alfie was so enwrapped in his conversation with Sammy that by the time his sister had finally chosen which magazine she wanted to get, and had arrived at the counter with Mrs Jones, he still hadn't asked for the pack of cards which he'd originally gone into the shop to buy.

For the remainder of the short walk

home from Sammy's shop, Alfie was much more like his normal self, constantly trying to trip his sister over and flicking her ear every time she mentioned his 'girlfriend' – which was often.

The reason behind Alfie's raised spirits was simple. He now knew just what he was going to do next.

That Saturday he would go and watch the Kingsway Harriers trials and while he was there he'd make sure to introduce himself to Lenny Fisher.

Chapter fifteen

The rest of that school week seemed to
drag on for even longer than usual.

By the time Saturday finally arrived, it
felt to Alfie like a month had passed since
he'd first learned about the Kingsway
Harriers trials due to be held that
afternoon; not four days.

It had said in the *Kingsway Courier*
that the trials were due to start at 12:30,
and as the Colts trained at the Kingsway
Recreation Ground every Saturday
morning until 12 o'clock, Alfie was
hopeful that he would be able to persuade
Billy's Dad to wait around for a while
after training – even though it was a cold
February morning and there was still a
slight overnight frost on the ground.

Those hopes, however, were swiftly dashed. Alfie had only just climbed into the back of Mr Morris's car when he'd been told that he and Billy would need to be ready to leave as soon as training finished, as Billy had to go and see his Nan and Grandad that afternoon.

Alfie tried not to let his disappointment show. After all, he reasoned, he could always ask one of the other parents for a lift home and try to convince them to stay and watch a bit of the trial. Liam's Dad usually stayed behind for a kickabout with Liam and Hayden after training anyway. Maybe he could go home with them instead?

Again though, his plan was quickly ruined.

"Liam's ill," said Hayden, who usually got a lift to training with him, when Alfie asked where the striker was. "My Mum had to bring me here this morning."

Alfie couldn't believe it. It was almost as though he was destined to never meet Lenny Fisher.

Before he had time to think about who he could ask next, Jimmy blew his whistle to signal the start of training.

The coach explained to his players what they would be doing during that morning's session and then sent them off on a lap around the pitch as part of their warm up.

However, before Alfie had a chance to set off, the coach called him over for a "quick chat."

"I don't suppose you saw the *Kingsway Courier* this week, Alfie? About the Kingsway Harriers?" the elderly coach asked.

Alfie smiled. Jimmy must have also seen the paper and spotted Lenny Fisher's name. He nodded. Then a thought crossed his mind. "Yeah, I saw it. Well, Sammy Reeves showed it to me. I don't suppose you're interested in staying to watch some of the trial after training, are you?"

Now it was Jimmy's turn to smile. "It's funny you should ask that. I was planning to hang around for a bit, actually."

"Do you mind if I stay with you? If you wouldn't mind giving me a lift home, that is? I'm sure my Mum and Dad won't mind as long as I phone and ask them first."

"That would be fine, Alfie. No problem whatsoever. But how are you going to phone them? The phone in that phone box over there is broken," said Jimmy, gesturing towards a public pay phone located by the recreation ground's car park.

"I'll just use my mobile," replied Alfie, sounding a little baffled by Jimmy's question.

The elderly coach laughed. He still wasn't used to the idea of ten year olds having mobile phones. If truth be told, he couldn't really get to grips with having a mobile phone himself. "Things certainly have changed since I was a youngster," he said, good-humouredly. "Then, yes, providing that's okay with your parents, I'd be happy for you to stay with me to watch the trial and then I'll take you home afterwards."

Alfie thanked Jimmy and then hurried off to phone his parents.

Like Alfie, Jimmy had also read the local newspaper's article about the Kingsway Harriers reforming with interest. What's more, like Alfie, Jimmy was also keen to talk to Lenny Fisher that afternoon.

However, Jimmy was not concerned with finding out why Lenny's name was printed on the card that Alfie had shown him almost a couple of weeks earlier. Instead he was keen to discover whether

116

the Harriers had any plans to set up their own youth system.

If Kingsway United weren't going to show any interest in the players that Jimmy suggested to them, then maybe Lenny Fisher would.

The elderly coach figured that if the Kingsway Harriers really were serious about once again becoming a professional team within the next five years, then by the time the likes of Billy and Hayden were old enough to play professional football, the Harriers should have already have achieved this aim. Therefore, if he could persuade Lenny to start up a youth system, then maybe his players could one day play for the Harriers.

Although Jimmy knew that both Billy and Hayden would rather play for United's Elite Centre, following his phone call to them a week earlier the Colts' coach guessed that there was little chance of this happening – at least not while Keith Johnson seemed to have some influence there.

Even though the Colts weren't due to have a match the following day, as it was their week off, Alfie was still buzzing during training. For the first time since he'd seen Madam Zola almost two weeks earlier he believed that he was finally close to finding out why the fortune teller had handed him that card with the strange badge and unknown name on it. With his mind clear, Alfie was fully focused on football throughout the session and even managed to outscore both Billy and Hayden during a passing, moving and shooting drill.

Because it was quite cold, Jimmy had decided to make sure the session was an active one, encouraging the players to keep moving as much as possible so that they could try and stay warm.

By the end of the session, nearly all of the Colts' players looked shattered. Only Ollie, who as ever had hardly done any running, and Alfie, who was far too excited to feel tired, seemed to have any energy left.

It took Jimmy, with assistance from Alfie, around 15 minutes to gather up all the various cones, bibs, poles and balls that they had used during the training session and then pack them into the back of his car.

Once they had done this and walked back over to the pitches, they could see that quite a few players had already arrived for the start of the trial, although

Alfie could see no sign of Lenny Fisher anywhere.

By 12:45, there were over 50 men standing around by the recreation ground's changing rooms, all dressed ready for the trial. But there was still no sign of anyone who seemed to be in charge.

Another ten minutes passed without anyone of any seeming importance turning up. Alfie could see that a good number of the men were starting to get fed up with waiting around and having no clue of what was supposed to be happening.

A few had already split themselves into two teams and were having an impromptu match with a ball that one of the men had fortunately brought with him, while others were slowly walking in the direction of their cars, ready to give up on the trial.

Jimmy was just about to suggest to Alfie that maybe they too should head off when finally an expensive looking black car pulled into the car park. Moments later a very old man, who both Jimmy and Alfie recognised as being Lenny Fisher thanks to the photo in the local paper, stepped, or rather shuffled, out of the car.

Within seconds, two younger men wearing training kits featuring the same badge that had been emblazoned on the card that Madam Zola had given to Alfie, got out of the back seats, took some items out of the boot of the car, and then started to follow Lenny towards the group of trialists.

"They must be the coaches," suggested Jimmy.

As Lenny walked wearily towards the group of men assembled by the changing rooms, Jimmy couldn't help but notice that he looked very, very well dressed. His grey suit was in perfect condition and his shiny black shoes looked brand-spanking new. Although Jimmy was no fashion expert, he was pretty sure that the suit and shoes would have cost Lenny a lot of money, while the car would have been astronomically expensive.

However, if you had of asked Alfie right there and then to describe just what Lenny was wearing, he wouldn't have been able to answer you.

He was too busy staring with disbelief at the person who had remained sitting in the car's passenger seat.

Chapter sixteen

Jimmy waited patiently for Lenny to finish addressing the players who had turned up for the trial.

Although the Colts' coach was standing too far away to hear what the Harriers' chairman was actually saying, judging by the impressed expressions on the faces of the trialists, Jimmy correctly guessed that he was probably outlining his ambitious plans for the team's future.

It didn't take a genius to work out, given the car he drove and the clothes he wore, that Lenny was an extremely wealthy old man.

Lenny Fisher spoke to the players for around five minutes before turning away, leaving the two coaches who had arrived with him, and who had been setting up some training areas while he'd been speaking, to start the trial.

Jimmy had expected Lenny to stay around to watch at least a little bit of the trial, but it soon became apparent that the chairman was not going to be hanging about. He was already heading straight for his car as fast as his elderly legs would allow.

"Excuse me. Mr Fisher, can I have a word?" Jimmy called out, as Lenny slowly hobbled past him.

"You're not a journalist, are you? I'm fed up with talking to reporters all the blooming time," Lenny replied grumpily, before turning to study Jimmy. "No. You don't look like a journalist. You look far too old to be a journalist."

While Jimmy didn't particularly mind being called old – after all, he was *quite* old – he thought that being called old by a man who was at least 10 years older than he was, was a tiny bit insulting.

"Erm, no. I'm not a journalist. Actually I'm a youth football coach."

"You definitely look too old to be a football coach," snapped Lenny, without so much as a pause.

Jimmy was briefly taken aback. He

wasn't used to being spoken to in such an abrupt manner by other adults. Well, apart from Keith.

"Well. What is it? What do you want? I haven't got time to be chatting to random old men in parks. I'm a very... no... I'm an extremely busy man."

Again, Jimmy was surprised by just how rude Lenny was.

Still, given his age, and the fact that trying to start a football team from scratch would be quite a stressful task for anyone, let alone for someone of Lenny's advanced years, Jimmy was prepared to let his rudeness slide on this occasion.

"Me and Alfie here were wondering if we could have a quick word with you. It won't take more than a few minutes." Jimmy gave Alfie a gentle nudge in the back to try and encourage him to join in the conversation.

However, the young boy was paying absolutely no attention whatsoever to either Jimmy or Lenny.

He was still too busy staring wide-eyed and open-mouthed at the person sitting in the car.

"I really don't have time for this. My son and I have a very important meeting this afternoon," said Lenny, sighing loudly.

"Look, take my card and give me a call in the week. I'll speak to you then."

Lenny handed Jimmy a business card, identical to the one that Madam Zola had given to Alfie in the wood by Danehill Park, and then stiffly turned away from them to continue his slow walk back to the car.

Jimmy studied the card for a moment, and then frowned. "But there's no phone number on here," he called. "It just says Lenny Fisher. Chairman of Kingsway Harriers."

Lenny just waved his hand dismissively and carried on walking, without once turning back round.

Jimmy shook his head sadly. He now knew that trying to talk to Lenny about setting up a youth system would undoubtedly be a waste of time.

"Well that didn't go quite as I'd hoped," he said to Alfie.

There was no response.

"Alfie. Alfie. Are you okay? You haven't said a word since Lenny arrived," said the old coach, shaking Alfie gently by the shoulder.

"The. The. Man," Alfie stuttered.

Jimmy looked at Alfie. An expression of pure confusion further wrinkling his

already heavily wrinkled face. "What man?"

"The man in the car." Alfie pointed in the direction of Lenny's flashy motor.

For the first time, Jimmy noticed that someone else had been sitting in the car. He peered at him for a few seconds, before saying, "I think I recognise him from somewhere."

Alfie nodded. "It's Tommy Fisher."

"Tommy who?"

The young boy quickly explained to his coach everything he'd found out about Tommy Fisher, how he'd seen him speaking to Keith at the Kingsway United match, and how he'd been sure

125

that Lenny and Tommy must be related.

Jimmy listened to everything that Alfie had to say. "That's where I recognise him from," he said, once Alfie had finished talking. "He was at last week's North Malling Town match. I saw him talking to Keith as I was walking past their pitch before our game."

Alfie nodded again. "I know. I saw him there, too. Do you think there's something strange going on?"

"No. I know there's something strange going on," the coach replied. "I've got a sneaky feeling that Tommy may just be the son that Lenny has an important meeting with this afternoon. Do you know if you're doing anything tomorrow?"

"Megan's got a street dancing competition, but I really don't want to go," Alfie answered, glumly. He hated Sundays when the Colts didn't have a match.

"Then ask your Mum and Dad if you can come with me tomorrow."

"Where to?"

"You'll see. Let's be off now," said Jimmy, gently ushering Alfie in the direction of his car. "I've got a very important phone call to make this afternoon."

Chapter seventeen

When Jimmy arrived to pick him up the following morning, Alfie still didn't have the slightest clue about where he was being taken or what he could expect to happen over the next few hours. Despite constant questions, Jimmy wouldn't tell him anything, either.

He already knew from past experience that Jimmy didn't like to share his plans with anyone else. However, he was fully confident that whatever it was the elderly coach had in mind, it would ultimately lead to them finding out the answers to all of their questions.

After all, it was thanks to one of Jimmy's plans that Keith and Jasper had left the Kingsway Colts 14 months earlier. Without him, Alfie would almost certainly not have still been playing for the Colts.

Yet Alfie was still surprised when, just a few minutes after getting into his car, Jimmy turned into the Kingsway Recreation Ground and parked in the car park.

"Why are we here?" he asked. "We don't have a match today."

"We may not have a game, but North Malling Town do. And I wouldn't be at all surprised if that means a certain Tommy Fisher will be here as well."

Sure enough, as Jimmy and Alfie briskly made their way towards North Malling's usual home pitch, they could see that Keith was deep in conversation with Tommy.

Jasper was there as well – as ever wearing his Kingsway United tracksuit. Alfie couldn't help but wonder whether that tracksuit had ever been washed since Jasper had been given it. He was *always* wearing it. It must have stunk more than a sweaty sumo wrestler's armpits!

Seconds later, Alfie noticed that another familiar face was standing on the sideline, ready to watch the game which hadn't yet kicked off. It was Reuben Ryan.

North Malling were playing Rickton Rovers and once again Reuben had turned up to watch his old teammates play.

Alfie gave Reuben a slight nod of his head by way of saying hello. It seemed to take Reuben a few moments to place just who Alfie was, and why he was nodding at him. However, after a brief pause, a look of recognition washed over his face and he returned the gesture.

Just as he had been the week before, Reuben was standing by himself doing various tricks with a football. Again, Alfie could only watch and marvel at how good Reuben was at using different parts of his body to keep the ball under control.

Alfie quickly noticed that Jasper, along with many of the other people there to watch the match, were also watching Reuben's performance.

After observing Reuben for a minute or two, Jasper decided that it was time to show all the watching adults and children just what he could do. Unfortunately for him, this wasn't very much.

Jasper had managed to keep the ball off the ground using his right foot just three times before he lost control of it. On his fourth touch he connected with the ball far too hard and sent it ballooning up into the air. The ball went up so high that Alfie thought that it would come down with snow on it.

Jasper charged after the ball as fast as he could in a desperate attempt to regain control of it.

He failed miserably.

The ball landed some five metres away from him, much to his obvious annoyance, and bounced towards where Jimmy and Alfie were standing. There was some light-hearted laughter from those who had witnessed Jasper's pitiful attempt to outdo Reuben, before they all turned back to watch his Academy teammate, who was now balancing the ball on his forehead.

As was customary for Jasper, he immediately started looking around for someone else to blame for his error. It was only then that he spotted Alfie for the first time.

"Why didn't you keep it up you muppet?" Jasper shouted, his face glowing an angry, and frankly rather unhealthy looking, shade of red. "Are you really that rubbish that you can't control a simple pass. It was obvious I was trying to pass to you. You really are useless!"

Alfie just rolled his eyes and said nothing. He was more than used to ignoring Jasper by now.

"What are you doing here anyway?" the larger boy snapped, realising that Alfie was not going to respond to being blamed for not keeping the ball in the air.

Again Alfie kept quiet. Not because he was ignoring Jasper, but because he didn't actually know why he was there. Jimmy still hadn't told him.

Jimmy was just about to answer, but before he could Keith had sauntered over to join his son.

"Well, well, well," North Malling's coach said gleefully, in his deep, booming voice. "Old man Jimmy Grimshaw and whatshisname Jones. Come to see how a real team plays have we?"

"Actually we played Rickton last week, so we already know how a real team plays," Jimmy answered smartly, before adding, "We're actually here to speak to Tommy Fisher."

For a moment Keith was taken aback. What reason could old man Grimshaw have for wanting to talk to Tommy?

He thought about it for a few seconds

131

before bursting into a fit of laughter. "Are you here to try and get Tommy to come and watch some of your games? You think you've got some players who are actually good enough to play for the Kingsway United Elite Centre or the Academy? Surely you don't mean young Jones here?" Keith chuckled again, pointing at Alfie.

"What's it to you why I want to speak to Tommy? What have you got to hide?" Jimmy responded, carefully eyeing Keith for a reaction.

Keith's reaction was to look genuinely confused. "Hide? Me? Nothing whatsoever, old man. I just know that when it comes to football, me and Tommy are on the same wavelength. He doesn't want to see all those weak, flashy players that play for you. He wants big strong, powerful boys, just like my Jasper."

A smile beamed across Jasper's face and he glanced at his Dad with a look of pure admiration.

"We've just been talking about that boy over there," Keith continued, pointing at Reuben. "Nothing but a flashy show-off. Always trying to make the other boys look silly with all his stupid little tricks and skills. I don't think he'll be

132

at Kingsway United much longer. Not Tommy's type of player at all."

"I shouldn't think he is," Jimmy agreed, before wandering off in Tommy's direction.

For a moment, Alfie found himself left alone with Jasper and Keith, but he quickly scampered off after his coach, intrigued to hear what Jimmy was actually going to say to Tommy.

Keith and Jasper also followed them. They were both equally keen to discover just what Jimmy wanted to talk to Tommy about.

"Tommy, can I have a quick word?" Jimmy asked, as he approached the manager of the Kingsway United Under 10s Elite Centre.

Tommy eyed the old man suspiciously. "Depends. Who are you?"

"My name is Jimmy Grimshaw. I'm the coach of the Kingsway Colts Under 10s."

"Oh, right," Tommy said disinterestedly. "Look, we're not actually looking for any new players at the moment. We're more than happy with what we've got – well almost," Tommy glanced quickly in the direction of Reuben, then back to Jimmy. "Maybe next season, yeah?"

"Well I'm not actually here to ask you

about looking at any of my players for next season. What I'd really like to know is why you're only selecting players who aren't very good for the Elite Centre and the Academy?"

"Oi," shouted Keith angrily. "You're talking rubbish, Grimshaw. My Jasper plays for the Academy."

Jimmy resisted the urge to thank Keith for helping him to prove his point, and instead stayed silent, continuing to stare evenly at Tommy.

"Well?" Jimmy pressed, after half-a-minute of silence.

Tommy laughed, nervously. "I don't know what you're talking about, old man.

Are you telling me that he's not a good player?" The Elite Centre's boss pointed towards Reuben.

"No. Not at all. In fact, I would say he's actually a very, very good player. Extremely skilful for his age. But I also know that you're thinking about getting rid of him."

Tommy's face flushed. "How do you know..." he began to ask, before glancing at Keith, who had started whistling. "Never mind. So what? Maybe he hasn't got exactly what I'm looking for. Who are you to question my selection policies?"

"Me?" Jimmy replied. "I'm no one. But he might be interested in what you've got to say." The Colts' coach pointed to a man who was talking to Reuben.

It was the man that Jimmy had phoned the previous afternoon.

Chapter eighteen

Having arrived home following his failed
attempt to talk to Lenny Fisher a day
earlier, Jimmy had once again decided
that a phone call to the Kingsway United
Elite Centre was in order.

He'd asked to speak to Tommy Fisher,
purely to check that he wasn't there,
and was promptly told by a bored
sounding woman that Tommy was out on
"important Academy business".

This was the exact response Jimmy had
expected – and hoped for. Tommy was the
one person Jimmy most certainly did not
want to speak to. He'd correctly guessed
that it must have been with Tommy to
whom he'd spoken the previous Saturday.

Jimmy then asked if he could speak to

whoever was in charge of overall youth development for Kingsway United. At first, the woman on the other end of the phone had been reluctant to give out any details, stating that Mr Murphy – the Head of Youth Development – was an extremely busy man and didn't have time to field calls from strangers.

Jimmy, however, was nothing if not persistent, and simply told the woman that he would only continue to keep calling and asking to speak to Mr Murphy for as long as it took him to get his desired outcome.

If the woman didn't believe him at first, she certainly did 30 minutes later, when Jimmy called for the fifth time. Sounding far more fed up than she had when Jimmy had first phoned, she eventually, if somewhat reluctantly, agreed to put him through to Ted Murphy.

Initially, Ted Murphy had not been at all happy to be interrupted, but as he listened to what Jimmy had to say he found himself becoming increasingly interested, and within minutes had agreed to meet the Kingsway Colts' coach for a coffee later that afternoon.

It was Ted Murphy whom Tommy Fisher now found himself looking at.

"Who's that?" asked Keith. "I'm sure I've seen him watching some of the Academy games."

"That's my boss," Tommy replied, through gritted teeth. "What's he doing here?"

"Maybe he's come to watch the game," said Jimmy, a huge smile spread right across his face.

Alfie was still extremely confused by everything that was going on.

Moments later, the match kicked off. Just as they had against the Colts during their previous game, Rickton dominated proceedings right from the kick off.

Their brand of quick, passing football and clever movement was just far too superior for North Malling's more direct hoof-it and hope approach. Unlike the game against the Colts, however, this time Rickton added goals to their dominance and by half-time they were 5-0 ahead.

Keith was so angry that he looked as though he was going to explode with rage at any minute.

During the half-time break, while Keith was yelling and screaming at his players in a misguided attempt to get them fired-up for the second half, Ted Murphy casually wandered over to join Alfie, Jimmy, Tommy and Jasper.

"Hello Tommy," he said, amiably.

"What are you doing here," Tommy blurted out in a panicked tone of voice, before quickly correcting himself. "I mean, good morning Mr Murphy."

"Good game this, isn't it?" Ted continued, as if Tommy hadn't spoken. "A lot of these Rickton Rovers players look quite useful. Actually, I'm quite surprised we haven't had some of them in for a trial. I'd say they were just the kind of players United are looking for, wouldn't you?"

"Well... erm... that's why I'm here this morning," Tommy just about managed to stutter. He sounded very unconvincing.

"Really?" mused Ted. "That's funny. I thought you were here to watch North Malling Town. I've heard that you seem to watch them most weeks."

Tommy blushed, but before he could say anything in response, Ted continued talking. "Thinking about it, didn't you used to play for North Malling?" he asked, turning to Jasper.

The boy nodded.

"Hmmm. And what do you think of Rickton Rovers?"

139

"Bunch of flashy muppets," replied Jasper. "If I was playing they wouldn't be winning 5-0. I'd have made sure of that. Couple of sneaky kicks here and there, they wouldn't know what had hit them," he added, cracking his knuckles for effect.

"Yes. Having seen you play I can quite believe that."

"Thanks," said Jasper enthusiastically, mistaking Ted's words for a compliment.

Shaking his head, Ted turned back to Tommy. "There's not that many, how shall I put it, really skilful players in the Under 10s Academy, is there Tommy?"

"Well... erm... there's... erm... there's him." Tommy pointed to Reuben, who was once again performing tricks on the side of the pitch.

"True," Ted agreed. "But if you remember, he was one of the few players that I personally called up to the Academy. I seem to remember a conversation with you only a few weeks ago when you told me he wasn't making the grade and you were thinking about letting him go. Not strong enough, I believe you said."

"Erm..." Tommy began, but again Ted interrupted him.

"In fact, if I was being honest, I'd go as

far to say that all the most skilful players in the Under 10s Academy have been selected by me."

"But Tommy selected me," interjected Jasper.

Ted looked at Jasper and smiled. "See, even the boy agrees with me."

A look of utter confusion swept across Jasper's face. Alfie couldn't stop a short burst of laughter escaping.

"How's your Dad, by the way?" Ted asked Tommy, seeming to completely change the topic of conversation.

"My... my Dad?" Tommy asked, sounding a little concerned by the change in subject.

"Yes, Tommy. Your Dad, Lenny. The chairman of the new Kingsway Harriers. You should remember him. You were sitting in his car yesterday afternoon."

"He's fine. Why?"

"Well. I met someone yesterday, thanks to this man," Ted patted Jimmy on the back. "Sammy Reeves he was called."

Shortly after Jimmy had dropped Alfie home the previous afternoon, and before he'd phoned the Elite Centre, the Colts' coach had popped into Sammy's shop. He had wanted to ask the shopkeeper what else he could remember about Lenny

141

Fisher. Fortunately, Sammy had been talking to some of his old friends about the 'good old days' earlier on in the week.

One of these friends had reminded Sammy that the Harriers had been relegated just a season after Lenny broke into the first team. He was never taken on by another club. His professional football career was over at just 19 years of age. All because Kingsway United came along and proved to be more successful than the Harriers.

Sammy told this story to Jimmy, who in turn relayed it to Ted over their afternoon coffee. Both men agreed that this would give Lenny – and maybe even his son – the perfect reason for hating United.

Ted now explained to Tommy what he had found out. When he'd finished, Tommy could barely contain his fury.

"My Dad was a great player," he erupted, angrily. "Everyone said so. But because Kingsway United came along, with their new ground and all their money, the Harriers couldn't compete. They were relegated and my Dad was left devastated. Heartbroken. He was never given another chance at a professional club!"

"So you got a job at the Kingsway

United Youth Development Centre and started to select players who you knew weren't good enough to ever make it professionally," said Ted, finishing Tommy's story for him. "You know lower league teams like United rely on their youth system so you decided to ruin it from within."

Tommy shrugged his shoulders, but stayed silent.

"But what about me!" Jasper shouted. He was visibly shaking. "You told my Dad I was good enough to make it. You said I was one of the most talented under 10s players you've ever seen. Were you... lying?" It took all of Jasper's willpower to stop his voice from cracking as he realised that Tommy had indeed been lying to him. He couldn't believe what he was hearing. Even Alfie felt a little bit sorry for him.

"I want your desk cleared first thing Monday morning," said Ted, jabbing a finger into Tommy's chest. "Now get out of my sight."

Tommy stormed off without saying another word.

Moments later Keith rejoined the rest of the group, having finally finished bawling at his players. "What's going on?"

he asked. "Where's Tommy going?" Keith then looked at his son. Jasper looked as though he was about to burst into tears. "Jasper? What's wrong?"

Jasper looked sadly up at his Dad, and then angrily turned to face Alfie. "This is your fault, muppet," he yelled. "I'm going to get you for this. Watch your back." With that, Jasper too stomped off in the direction of the car park, Keith quickly following after him, still trying to find out what had happened.

That left Jimmy, Alfie and Ted standing by themselves on the sideline.

"I'm glad you called me yesterday," said Ted, shaking Jimmy by the hand. "I'd suspected something wasn't right for some time. But I'm so busy with all the other teams at the Development Centre that I don't get a chance to spend as much time as I'd like overseeing things. It was only when you told me about Tommy's connection to Lenny Fisher that I started to realise what was going on."

Jimmy smiled. "Well, it's Alfie you really should be thanking," he said. "It was him who found out most of the information. I just put the finishing touches together. Just think, Alfie, if you hadn't have found that card in the wood and started asking questions about it then we probably would never have ended up finding any of this out. Tommy's plan might have worked and in a few years time United could have been in real trouble. Most people would have just thrown the card away, or not picked it up in the first place. It's a good job you kept it, hey?"

Alfie nodded, but stayed silent. He was going over everything that had happened in his mind. He knew that Madam Zola had given him the card for a reason; to make his destiny come true he needed Tommy Fisher out of the Kingsway United Youth set-up!

As ever, the fortune teller was helping him to keep his dream of becoming a professional footballer on track – albeit in her own cryptic style.

"Anyway," continued Ted, "all of this means that we're now short of an Under 10s head coach at the Elite Centre." He looked fixedly at Jimmy.

"You mean me..." the elderly coach exclaimed, obviously totally shocked by the suggestion.

Alfie's smile stretched from ear to ear. If there was one thing he knew Jimmy most certainly would be, were he to accept the job, it was fair.

Chapter nineteen

Alfie usually hated speaking to anyone
on his mobile phone. His phone
conversations tended to last no longer
than half a minute and seemed to
consist of him making a series of slightly
different grunting noises.

Yet Mr and Mrs Jones were constantly
amazed at how he would finish the call
having organised a full set of plans with
his friends.

They figured it must be down to a
specially-devised grunting language
known only to children.

That Sunday night, however, Mr and
Mrs Jones had to use all their powers
of persuasion to stop Alfie from phoning
everyone in his contacts list. He'd already

spent two hours on the phone, speaking to Billy, Hayden, Chloe and Liam, and telling them about everything that had happened earlier that morning, before Mr Jones finally convinced Alfie to go and get ready for bed and tell the rest of his friends at school the next day. The promise of two packets of football cards no doubt helped Alfie agree to his parents increasingly desperate pleas.

Megan had taken great delight in hearing Alfie talking to Chloe on the phone. But even his little sister's stupid songs and annoying rhymes didn't bother him on that particular evening. He was in a great mood.

When Liam pointed out that if Jimmy did choose to accept the Kingsway United Elite Centre job then he would no longer be able to coach the Colts, Alfie's mood had soured momentarily. But he quickly brushed away any concerns. He'd spent the entire afternoon thinking about what had transpired that morning and had come to the conclusion that Jimmy was supposed to get the job. That was the exact outcome Madam Zola had planned – it was the real reason she had given him that card.

Settling down in bed a little bit later

on, Alfie started to think about what it would be like to join the Elite Centre – and then one day play for the Academy and eventually the Kingsway United first team!

While Alfie knew that Jimmy wouldn't pick him for a trial unless he really deserved it, and he begrudgingly accepted that players such as Billy, Hayden and Reuben were all still technically better than him at the moment, he also believed that if he could improve, then Jimmy would be only too happy to have him in the Elite Centre.

Alfie was just starting to drift off to sleep, imagining what it would be like to pull on the famous blue and white Kingsway United shirt, when he heard a familiar sound.

Wind chimes.

Alfie sat bolt upright in his bed and remained motionless for a few moments, waiting to see if he would hear the noise again.

He didn't have to wait too long. Within seconds he heard the unmistakable tinkling sound again. Louder this time.

The noise was coming from just outside his bedroom door. Intrigued, Alfie inched slowly out of his bed and crept as quietly as he could along his bedroom floor, taking the utmost care to avoid the various magazines, football cards and lego bricks which, as ever, were strewn all over the carpet.

Quietly, he pressed down on the handle, opened the door and stepped out into the hallway. Immediately he was met with a gust of cold air. It was freezing.

Alfie looked about him and instantly saw that he was not standing in his hallway. Once again the landing had completely disappeared. Instead, he was back in the exact same wood he had found himself in just over two weeks earlier.

This time, however, he didn't feel scared or nervous. He felt excited.

As Alfie made his way steadily along the wood's path, desperately hoping to avoid standing on a sharp twig as he had last time, the sound of the wind chimes grew louder and louder.

After a few minutes of walking he reached the far end of the wood and upon doing so the noise of the wind chimes immediately stopped.

The young boy looked all around him, but couldn't see anything out of the ordinary (well, aside from the fact his house's hallway had turned into a wood, that is).

Feeling confused and disappointed, Alfie quietly called out, "Madam Zola? Madam Zola? Are you here?"

There was no answer.

He tried again, a little louder this time, but again the result was the same. There was no reply.

Suddenly something jumped onto the path and scuttled quickly between Alfie's legs, causing him to jump and almost scream out loud.

After taking a few moments to calm himself and get his heartbeat back to something approaching a normal speed, Alfie turned around to see what it was that had jumped out at him.

It's fair to say that he wasn't all that surprised to see a squirrel.

As soon as Alfie looked at it, the squirrel started running again, back in the direction from which he had just come. Alfie decided to try and follow it and had to jog to keep the squirrel in his sights – a job that was made all the more difficult by the fact it was so dark he could barely see past the end of his nose and that he was bare-footed.

He seemed to have been running for

ages when the squirrel finally stopped, jumped off the path and climbed up the nearest tree. "Well I'm not following you up there, if that's what you want," Alfie said aloud, feeling slightly foolish to be talking to a squirrel.

It was only then that Alfie noticed that there was someone else in the wood. Standing in the middle of two trees some distance away, he could clearly make out the silhouette of a person. Alfie knew immediately who it was.

"Madam Zola," he shouted at the top of his voice.

The silhouette waved to him and then lifted their other wrist, as if checking the time.

Alfie put his head down and started running as fast as he possibly could towards the person.

However, by the time he reached the two trees, which were located on either side of the path at the point where he had entered the wood, Madam Zola was gone. Disappointedly, Alfie stepped off the path, hoping he would be able to catch a glimpse of the direction in which she'd gone.

However, the very second that Alfie stepped off the path, the trees disappeared and he found himself standing back in his bedroom doorway.

Feeling confused, disappointed and, most of all, extremely tired, Alfie decided there was nothing else to do right now but to go back to bed. No doubt he'd see Madam Zola again one day, when she next had a task, or some advice, for him.

He shut his bedroom door quietly behind him and then quickly flung it open again. Everything was back to normal. He crept into the hallway just to make sure, and was soon satisfied that there were no trees anywhere to be seen.

Once again he entered his bedroom and closed the door. He turned to move in the direction of his bed, but succeeded only in accidently kicking over one of the many piles of football cards that was on his floor.

He was going to just leave them there and pick them all up in the morning – probably – when something made him stop.

Although it was dark, a slither of moonlight that was coming through a tiny gap in his curtains was illuminating one of the cards that he'd just knocked over. It was a card he'd never seen before.

He picked it up and studied it intently,

turning it over and over in his hands, before smiling. The card featured a Kingsway United player, but Alfie couldn't tell who it was as the player had no face. Scribbled on the back of the card, though, in handwriting he didn't recognise, were two words. 'Alfie Jones?'

Alfie quickly surmised that Madam Zola must have put the card in his room – that's why she had lured him away from his bedroom. He smiled again, put the card in the top draw of his bedside table and clambered into bed. He was asleep the moment his head hit the pillow.

That night, Alfie dreamt, as ever, of becoming a professional footballer.

This time, though, the dream seemed a little bit more real than it ever had before.